deadly
devotion
ELAINE OVERTON

KIMANI
ROMANCE

To George,
The strength of a Grizzly,
and the heart of a Teddy.
Never change

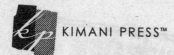

KIMANI PRESS™

ISBN-13: 978-0-373-86022-7
ISBN-10:   0-373-86022-6

DARING DEVOTION

Copyright © 2007 by Elaine Overton

This is a work of fiction. Names, characters, places and incidents are
either the product of the author's imagination or are used fictitiously,
and any resemblance to actual persons, living or dead, business establishments,
events or locales is entirely coincidental.

www.kimanipress.com

Printed in U.S.A.

Dear Reader,

I hope you have enjoyed Cal and Andrea's story. This one has been a long time in coming, and it is because I wanted to be able to aptly express the challenges presented to them. In researching this story, I was surprised by how many people actually suffer from post-traumatic stress disorder, and how disabling this condition can be.

Cal and Andrea not only had to overcome Cal's PTSD, but Andrea's fear of losing the man she loved. I write fiction, but Andrea's fear is the very real fear of thousands of spouses around the world.

As I'm sure you all have realized with *Love's Inferno* and now *Daring Devotion*, I have a great admiration for firefighters, what they do and the challenges of their chosen occupation. I hope I have been able to give you a realistic glimpse into the lives of these very uncommon people in an entertaining and informative way.

Please feel free to contact me at www.elaineoverton.com; I truly enjoy reading your e-mail. Thank you!

Elaine Overton

Chapter 1

Firehouse Fifteen
Detroit, Michigan

"Hail to the Chief!"

Andrea Chenault sat quietly with a smile frozen on her face. She sat beside her fiancé, Calvin Brown, more lovingly known by his friends as Big Cal, and listened in wooden silence as he was saluted and cheered on his recent promotion to Firehouse Chief.

In the midst of the lively celebration, Andrea's mind was swirling with doubt and turmoil regarding the future of her engagement.

Feeling Cal's eyes dart across her face, she took a sip of soda, studying the pretty design on the side of the Dixie paper cup to avoid making eye contact as Dwight Johnston, their friend and Cal's fellow fireman, continued his toast.

What Cal's engine team members saw as nothing more than the culmination of a lifetime of hard work and commitment, Andrea saw as an omen of bad things to come.

Dwight lifted his paper cup in salute. "It couldn't have happened to a better man. Here's to Big Cal!"

Cheerful affirmatives came from the men and women crowded around the table in the small firehouse kitchen. Andrea could only hope that no one noticed that the one person who should've been happiest for Cal was unable to muster even a fraction of enthusiasm.

Others rose and offered their own congratulations, many recounting events in which Cal had proven his heroism, and there was also the occasional funny story until eventually their celebration dinner evolved into an impromptu roast.

Andrea tried not to watch the clock, but she

was really uncertain as to how much more of the incessant merriment she could take. Consciously, she toyed with the engagement ring on her finger, twisting it back and forth as her mind ran away with the possibilities. A large, warm hand covered hers and stopped the motion of the ring. She looked up into Cal's concerned brown eyes.

What's wrong? he silently pleaded, and Andrea just shook her head in answer, hoping he would not push.

"Speech! Speech!" the crowd cried for some words from their new leader.

With one more look in Andrea's general direction, Cal slowly unbent his large frame from the table, and Andrea felt the same tinkling sensation in the pit of her stomach that she felt every time she took in his exceptional form.

At six feet, four inches, Calvin Brown was a three hundred-pound slab of solid granite, covered in a top layer of milk chocolate skin. Although he'd been a fireman his entire adult life, he was often mistaken as a professional body builder by strangers. His perfectly sculpted body was the product of years of weight lifting and various training programs. He took great pride in his ability to lift twice his own weight.

Although Cal was a large man, his size was not what made him unique. It was the strength and brawn that could be felt in the slightest handshake, and yet, despite his size, he moved with the agility of a dancer. And had an innately gentle nature that told you that his strength would never be misused.

He tapped the side of his paper cup with a plastic spoon in a dramatic gesture to gain everyone's attention, and the room quieted down.

"I know many of you may be wondering if this promotion will change me in any way," he began with a solemn expression. "I would just like to state for the record that now that I am your chief, I am still the Big Cal you've always known and loved."

Cal continued his speech, despite the laughter in the background. "Now, I know some of you may be bitter…" the group laughed again, "but believe me, the forces that be picked the best man or woman for the job and you'll just have to get over it."

Ignoring the playful hoots and boos, Cal smiled graciously, exposing one his few physical imperfections, the two front teeth that slightly overlapped his bottom ones.

Instead of finding it unattractive, Andrea had

loved his bucktoothed smile from the moment she saw it. She always thought it gave his face a boyish appeal.

He cleared his throat loudly to be heard over the laughter and noise. "As I was saying, this promotion will not change the man I am." He paused thoughtfully. "But, in regards to work assignments, I would like to add that I *am* open to flattery, and *not* above bribery."

The group roared in laughter.

Andrea's eyes scanned the room seeing nothing but smiling faces filled with genuine admiration and respect. She knew in their own way, these people loved him as much as she did. And yet, collectively, she couldn't help but see them as the enemy. Her primary point of contention as far as she could see was that the thing they loved and admired most about him was the one thing Andrea wished she could change.

Unable to stand it any longer, Andrea whispered in Cal's ear that she was going to the bathroom. She quickly hurried out of the room, never knowing Cal's eyes followed her until she disappeared through the doorway.

Once outside in the hallway, she leaned her back against the wall and took a deep breath.

She never realized how exhausting holding a fake smile for hours could be.

She heard someone ask Cal if she was okay, but she could not make out Cal's murmured response through the thick wall. Taking another deep breath, she started down the hall, hoping that a splash of water on her face would help hold back the tears that now seemed to threaten her constantly.

A few minutes later, as she stood at the sink patting her face dry, she silently scolded the woman in the mirror. *This is the happiest day of his life and you are going to ruin it for him. Pull yourself together!*

She glanced down at the small diamond ring on her finger, and her hand went to it instinctively as she remembered just how many times over the past week she'd taken it off and put it back on.

She pulled it off once more, enclosed it in her small fisted hand. "I'm not this strong," she whispered, imagining the day her telephone would ring and there would be a composed, very professional voice at the other end informing her of their regret...

She turned and leaned her back against the sink. As a nurse, Andrea had seen more death than most people saw in a lifetime, and many of those were lives that seemed to be snuffed out before their time.

She'd stood over the body of more than one firefighter as the line on the ventilator went flat, and found it far too easy to imagine Cal as the firefighter on the table.

"I'm not strong enough to be a fireman's wife." But despite her words, she found herself sliding the little ring back onto her finger. She only hoped she could hide her dismay long enough to get through the afternoon.

She checked her appearance in the mirror before she opened the door and found herself facing an expanse of black T-shirt stretched across a wide, muscular chest.

Closing her eyes, Andrea breathed in his familiar scent of soap and Speed Stick deodorant. Cal almost never wore cologne, and Andrea found that she preferred it that way. His own natural scent was enough of an aphrodisiac by itself.

"What's wrong?" Cal's deep baritone voice was softened by his concern.

Her eyes went up and up until they settled on soft brown eyes filled with concern. She tried to force a smile, but when she felt the tears welling up, she quickly looked away.

"Nothing's wrong."

"Don't lie to me." His tone never changed, but there was something very threatening in the words themselves. "You look like you're about to cry."

She shook her head fervently. "No, I'm okay. We better get back to the group—they're going to wonder where the guest of honor disappeared to." She moved to go around him, and he easily blocked her path.

"They can wait." Using his index finger, he lifted her chin, and although she managed to keep her eyes downcast, the tiny drop of water that fell on her cheek betrayed her.

She heard his sharp gasp right before he pulled her into a rough embrace. "Baby, why are you crying? Tell me."

She eagerly wrapped her arms around his rock-hard midsection and held on with all her might. Not yet ready to share the truth…that she was seriously considering giving him back his ring because she could not bear to be his widow.

Holding him in her arms proved to be too much. Faced with the possibility of having to let him go, the water began coursing down her face.

"Andrea, you're going to have to tell me, I can't read your mind. What's got you so upset?"

She pressed her face against his shirt and tried to stifle the flood of tears. She wasn't ready to say the words. Not yet...*not yet.*

The loud, buzzing sound that signaled an emergency call reverberated throughout the firehouse, and without hesitation Cal set Andrea away from him. With one quick peck on her forehead, he whispered the words "You know what to do." And then he was gone.

Andrea stood in the deserted hallway, listening to the quiet firehouse come to life around her. Cal was right. After a year of being his girlfriend and fiancée, Andrea did know what to do.

He'd trained her in civilian procedure and protocol during an emergency as well as he trained his engine team to respond. They even ran through the occasional drill.

Andrea knew everything she needed to know to be a fireman's wife...except how to stop the uncontrollable shaking she felt take over her body every time the firehouse alarm rang. She turned and hurried back along the hall, trying to focus on the task assigned to her, and not the danger Cal was rushing into.

* * *

Once the corridor was quiet, the man crouching in the shadows stepped out from his hiding place. Jeff Collins looked in both directions before heading down the back stairway toward the soon departing engine truck.

Nothing would appear more suspicious than for him to not be on the truck when it pulled away from the firehouse. For a moment, he'd been extremely worried, wondering if the woman would stand there until it was too late, but finally she'd moved off down the hall.

When Cal got up and left the table, Jeff Collins had followed, curious to see what would transpire between the couple. His lips tightened as he remembered the sadness in Andrea's eyes as Cal was praised and toasted. Jeff was no happier to see Cal get the promotion than Andrea.

His fist balled at his side as he remembered how close he'd come to being the one toasted and praised. It just wasn't fair. He and Cal had been equals since entering the firefighter academy fifteen years ago, both at the tender age of nineteen. They'd both had distinguished careers. So, why, when it came time to pass out the promotions, was Cal the only man to get one?

Over the past five years, Jeff Collins had maneuvered his way through the ranks, manipulating and cajoling his way up the professional ladder, only to have the prize stolen out from under him in the eleventh hour. Calvin Brown had *stolen* his promotion.

A promotion, a beautiful fiancée…it just wasn't fair. He slipped on his turn-out gear and swung up into the truck just as the garage door began lifting.

"Where the hell have you been?" Cal's voice boomed, drowning out even the sound of the horn warning.

Jeff fought to hide his anger, and swallowed hard. "Sorry, got hung up."

"Don't let it happen again." Cal slammed the front wall to signal the driver that everyone was aboard. "Let's go."

Without further warning, the truck began to pull forward, maneuvering its way through the traffic that had come to a complete halt.

Jeff focused on the view of the city flying by, while Cal conversed with Dwight. At times like this, it took everything in him to hide the growing hatred he felt for the man he'd once considered a friend.

Chapter 2

The heat was suffocating. Flames of orange, red and gold danced around him in menacing cadence, teasing and taunting mercilessly. But nothing could sway Cal's attention from the small figure clutching the wall on the other side of the room.

When he'd first spotted the child, he could not believe his eyes. It was Marco, one of the many neighborhood children who hung around the firehouse with hero worship in their young eyes. Cal hadn't seen him in several days, but now here he was in the midst of an out-of-control blaze in the abandoned Hadley Building, a condemned former office complex in the heart of downtown.

Cal took in the gaping hole in the center of the floor as his mind constructed a way around it. "Hang on, Marco, I'm coming!" He slid slowly to the right, trying not to disturb the fragile, burnt wood surrounding the hole. If it got any bigger, he would never reach the other side.

"Cal? Cal is that you?" Marco lifted his head from his crouched position, recognizing the voice of the firefighter. "Help me, Cal!"

"I'm coming, little man, just hang on!"

He moved with care and precision, his eyes darting between the opening in the floor and the small, terrified creature on the other side

By the time he was twelve years old, Cal was as tall and broad as an average sized adult male. An anomaly that had been both a blessing and curse. His size had kept the bullies at bay—after all, no one challenged a six foot seventh grader—but he also realized that he did not fit in the usual places that kids his age did, and soon became the butt of jokes and teasing.

To counter what he felt was his own clumsiness, he became very conscious of his movements. Even now, he could almost move with the stealth of a ninja. This skill had served him well in his line of work, especially at times like this when a lack of movement was critical to success.

Moving along the wall, he came to a corner and edged around it until there was only a small space that he had to cross in order to reach Marco. He shifted on the ball of his left foot to leap across the gaping abyss. He made the leap and landed only inches from Marco, but behind him the floor disappeared, burning away until only six inches of floor remained behind him.

He scooped the feather-light child up in his arms, and turned to put his back against the wall. He surveyed his options, and realized there were none. He could not go back the way he'd come because the cavity in the floor had widened so that it was almost impossible to cross. Even if they made it, the surrounding wood was so fragile it probably would not support their weight.

On his other side, the fire was eating its way through anything in its path and heading straight for them. Cal knew then that he had no choice but to try to leap across the opening, and *hope* that they made it. The only other option would be wait for the fire to consume them.

He shifted the boy around so he could look at his face. "Marco, I'm going to put you on my back. I need to have my hands free to hang on once we make the jump."

"Jump?"

Hearing the panic in his voice, Cal knew he had to act quickly, before the boy had a chance to scare himself into refusing to cooperate. He pushed his small body around and over his shoulder, didn't have to tell him to hang on. Marco was already clinging to him like a spider monkey.

"No matter what, don't let go!" Cal said, taking the fateful leap just seconds before the flames covered the wall they'd been leaning against.

The next few seconds happened so slowly, Cal felt as if he were experiencing some kind of a weird dream. He could see the ledge on the other side, and then suddenly it was no longer there and they were free falling through space.

Down into the abyss of a swirling river of flames that covered the lower levels of the building. Suddenly, Cal felt something clamp down hard on the collar of his rubber jacket, and he realized he was suspended in midair.

"Hang on, Cal! I've got you!" Even muffled

by her oxygen mask, Cal recognized the voice of Marty, the only female member of the team.

He felt himself being towed upward, one inch—stop. The movement started again, another half inch—then, one hard yank. She relaxed her stance to catch her breath, and her heavy burden slipped back down three inches.

"Get the boy!" Cal called, his voice infused with fear as he felt the boy's tight little clawlike nails losing their hold. "He's slipping! Get the boy first!"

Marty reached over his shoulder and lifted the small burden. The child went willingly as Marty sat him behind her. Then she went back to trying to lift the much heavier man.

Cal felt his spirit plummet. Marty was more than capable of pulling her weight—but not his. Cal could feel himself slipping even more, slowly and steadily out of her sweaty grip. He knew that as sure as the sun rose in the morning, Marty would never let go of him, which meant she would go over the side with him. He couldn't let that happen.

"Let me go, Marty!" he shouted through his fogged mask. "Let me go!"

"No!"

He came up an inch.

"No!"

He came up another inch. Trembling with the effort, she relaxed her exhausted muscles just a fraction, and he slipped back down a half inch.

She can't do it, Cal thought, and somehow, someway, he had to make her let him go.

He looked down into the nothingness beneath him. The wide opening of burnt wood that spiraled down at least twenty feet left him feeling as if he were staring into hell. Instantly he realized he'd made a critical mistake.

A *swirling* hell…vertigo.

"Take the boy and get out of here!" he shouted, but when he felt her continuing to pull, he knew he was being ignored.

His head felt light, as beads of sweat popped out on his face beneath his oxygen mask. Without thought, his large feet began swinging back and forth trying to find purchase on one of the many, jagged levels that had not burned completely away. He knew he should've just held still, but panic had taken hold of his brain.

"Cal, stop! I'm losing you!"

The fire burned below, the orange and red flames dancing in anticipation of the feast of flesh it was about to devour. The heat surrounding him, inside and outside of his suit had him near fainting, something he'd never done in his entire life.

The tip of one foot reached a small, solid foundation just another inch below him. He experimented with putting pressure on the surface. Cal was certain if he could just get his foot firmly on the small, unburned portion of the next level, he could get clear of the opening.

He pushed his body in the direction he wanted to go. His only consolation was that if this did not work, the fall would kill him before the fire ever reached him. Even in death, he refused to give the monster its due.

Cal's foot touched on the landing just as the wood surrendered to the inferno. His body slid and scraped along the jagged edge until his fingers hooked onto something that felt like a handle and he broke the fall. Using both hands to hold, he tried to lift his heavy form up and over the ledge. Even though the edge had broken away, most of the charred landing was still in place.

As Cal hung dangling from the edge, he realized it was times like this when a man would be tempted to question God. Death at the hands of the very monster he'd spent his life working to defeat just didn't seem right.

And what about Andrea? He could clearly see her beautiful face. Big brown eyes filled with more compassion than he'd ever imagined existed. Her golden-brown skin. Her cute little up-turned nose and full lips. He'd waited his whole life for a woman like her and now he would lose her, as well. He should've married her a year ago, when he first proposed. Why had he waited so long?

"Cal! You down there?" He heard a man's muffled voice coming from somewhere above. It was Dwight. Marty had gone for help. Cal could sense more than see the group of firefighters peering over the edge a few feet above. He was too exhausted to speak, but he had to find the strength, otherwise his team would believe him dead.

"Yeah, I'm still here," he called back and tried to lift his weight over the edge.

"Hang on! We're coming!" Dwight called down into the opening.

Cal tried to lift his body again, and managed to get his left shoulder up over the edge. He hung, listening to the crackling wood and running feet. The feeling of helplessness was a new sensation. *And not a pleasant one,* Cal thought.

This blaze was probably the worst they'd seen in some time, and the closest he'd ever come to meeting the Grim Reaper. Cal felt large, strong arms clamp around his torso and start to pull him up. Then other hands grabbed the back of his jacket and hauled him over the edge. Tommy took him under the arms while Jeff grabbed his legs and pulled up and over. The pair quickly rolled his large body back away from the edge.

"We've got him!"

From somewhere in the distance, he heard Dwight calling. "Let's go! I can't hold it much longer. Let's go!" Dwight had been busy trying to secure an exit route for his team.

"Where's Marco?" He looked in every direction, before noticing the small bundle tucked in Marty's arms.

Braced between Jeff and Tommy, Cal used his own legs to run out of the building, despite his dizziness and nausea. A rhythmic bumping noise behind them signaled the others had caught up.

Following the path made by Dwight, the group quickly found the back entrance and exited into the empty alley. In the distance Cal could see the lights of an ambulance flashing, as well as the firemen's ladder truck, and a couple of police vehicles. He found himself being twisted this way and that as Marty satisfied herself that her friend was still in one piece. The sound of scanners and radios were emanating from every direction.

Jeff tried to help guide him to the paramedics, who were now coming down the long alley to meet them halfway. Cal allowed the man to brace him as he watched the world spinning around him.

Cal took off his helmet and mask and shook his head hard, trying to dispel the feeling of vertigo that seemed to be lingering. He felt more than a little nauseous, and pushed Jeff away as he felt himself becoming sick.

Before the paramedics reached them, Cal turned toward the brick wall, and shielded himself as best as he could while emptying his stomach, his head spinning, his stomach churning. His friends closed in with worried expressions.

Unable to stand any longer, Cal leaned his back against the wall and hung his head in complete exhaustion.

He heard the paramedics quietly discussing the best way to transport their large victim. Then the stretcher appeared and Cal was laid out across it. He closed his eyes to stop the white clouds from spinning overhead.

"We'll meet you at the hospital." He heard Dwight in the distance. With his other team members wishing him well, the paramedics rolled Cal back to the ambulance and loaded him.

As the doors on the vehicle closed and Cal heard the siren sound, he silently wondered what was wrong with him. He'd been prone long enough to have regained some sense of equilibrium. But still he felt as if the world was spinning around him and he had no gravity.

He watched the technicians go about their routine, inserting the IV and dispensing the necessary medications. He answered their questions as best he could with head shakes and nods. He took a deep breath and decided that whatever was wrong would soon correct itself. He was Big Cal, nothing kept him down for long, not even a near-death experience.

He closed his eyes and thanked God for another miracle, the latest in a long line. His mind went to Andrea. He desperately needed to see her, to hold her, to know that she was real because that would mean that he was real. That he was still alive in all the ways that mattered.

Chapter 3

"Cal." Andrea scooted up on her knees to use her full strength to rock the man beside her as he thrashed about wildly on the bed. "Cal!" She ducked, barely missing a swinging arm. "Cal! Wake up!" She pushed hard against his tense form. "Wake up!"

Large eyes opened in bewilderment. "What?" Cold brown eyes turned to her and the lack of recognition sent a chill down her spine.

"It was a nightmare." She rubbed her hand along his jawbone. "You were having another nightmare."

He looked in every direction seemingly surprised to find himself in her bed. Finally his troubled eyes settled on her again just before he ran his large hand over his face.

It had been almost a month since the fire in the Hadley building, and something deep inside of Cal had changed. Andrea sensed it and saw it in his behavior. In the past few days, Andrea had seen something she thought she would never see. Her fearless man had become hesitant.

Andrea had met Cal over a year ago, although she remembered it like yesterday. He'd come to visit Marty in the hospital where she was recovering from smoke inhalation. From the moment Andrea saw him, Cal had exuded a kind of larger-than-life confidence, and being the self-doubting person that she was, Andrea had been drawn to that self-assuredness. She'd known instinctively that he was everything she'd never known she needed, water to her parched soul.

Over the past year, they'd struggled to find their way through the complex maze of contemporary relationships and had seemingly come to the inevitable conclusion that they belonged together.

When Cal had proposed almost six months ago, her instant answer had been yes. And on that day something strange had happened to Andrea. Something that she was finding harder and harder to deal with. For the first time, she began to contemplate what it meant to be the wife of a firefighter. What she'd discovered was not good.

The never-ending sense of dread. The empty feeling that settled in the pit of her stomach every time he began a seventy-two-hour rotation. The feeling would not go away until he returned to her after a call, safe and sound. And the apprehension had not stopped there. It followed her to work where, as a nurse in the emergency ward, she became more aware of the number of firefighters that came through the E.R.

And on one horrible day, less than a month ago, she'd had her worst fears confirmed when she looked down at the gurney and saw that Cal was the patient. But something strange and wonderful had come out of the experience, something Andrea could not share with anyone, not even Cal. Something she was ashamed to admit gave her such pleasure. Cal had lost his sense of invincibility.

She could remember any number of times she'd been in the firehouse when the emergency call came in and Cal would take off with a sexy

grin and the wink of an eye, excited and pumped
for the challenge. It was all she could do to wait
for him to leave before she dropped to her knees
and began to pray. Cal absolutely loved fighting
fire.

It was the greatest obstacle in their path and
the one thing Andrea thought was unchangeable.

But since the Hadley building fire, that wickedly playful gleam had left his eyes. He'd
doubled the drills for his team. He'd become
careful, and Andrea knew there was nothing as
dangerous as an overly cautious firefighter.
Which meant…he'd have to give it up. Now, all
she had to do was wait for him to realize it.

"Do you want to talk about it?" she asked
quietly, already knowing the answer before he
shook his head and rolled over.

Almost every night he'd spent with her since
the accident had been the same. She'd wake him
in the middle of a nightmare, and he'd shrug it
off as nothing, roll over and go back to sleep.

"Why won't you talk to me?"

"About what?" he mumbled into the pillow.

"About the fire. About what really happened."

"I told you a thousand times, baby, nothing
happened."

"Is this…" She hesitated. More than once he'd snapped at her when she attempted to ask questions regarding exactly what happened. "Because of Marco?"

Marco had recently been released from the hospital. He'd had to stay longer than Cal to have a skin graft covering a six-inch patch of burnt skin on his arm. But given what could've happened, Andrea thought, the boy had been incredibly blessed.

Of course, Cal had taken full responsibility for that, as well. "You saved his life, Cal, the skin graft was a small price compared to—"

"I don't want to hear it, Andrea! You weren't there—you don't know what you're talking about!"

A cold silence settled over the dark room.

Sometimes Andrea felt as if she was trying to cuddle up to a wounded bear. She sighed in defeat and turned back over to her side of the bed and snuggled under the covers.

She stared at the wall seeing right through the darkness. She studied the outline of the soft pink watercolor painting of a vase of peonies. Once again, her mind was swirling with conflicting emotions, many of which she knew she shouldn't feel. Even in the midst of Cal's crisis some part of her was blossoming with hope. There was no way he could go back to being a firefighter, not in his current state of mind.

And as much as Andrea hurt for him, as much as it pained her to see him in such turmoil, some part of her still preferred it to the *who-gives-a-damn* way of looking at the world he had before. That attitude was dangerous, reckless, and…ultimately fatal.

After several minutes, Cal turned over to spoon her. His large hand came over her hipbone and settled in the crook of her body. Although Andrea sensed the movement wasn't meant to be arousing, she had no control over the tinkling sensation that started in her toes and worked its way up her body. It had been that way from the beginning. The most casual skim of his hand, an accidental brush of bodies and she was wired for action.

Cal was the first man she'd ever known who had that kind of effect on her senses, and in her heart she knew he would always be the only one who could.

"I'm sorry," he whispered in the dark. "I didn't mean to snap at you like that."

She sighed. "No, it's my own fault. As many

times as you've told me to leave it alone, you think I'd give up."

He snuggled in closer, wrapping his large body around hers. "Don't ever give up on me, baby. No matter how much like a jackass I behave." He squeezed her against him so quickly and so tight Andrea could barely breath, and just as quickly he released his viselike hold. "Don't ever give up on me."

Andrea said nothing. His words were too close to her fretful contemplations.

Cal propped himself up on one elbow. "Look, what happened to me is nothing new, it comes with the job. The bad dreams—all that will stop eventually. It's just that it is still fresh in my mind. I'll be fine."

She turned to face him. "So, it has nothing to do with feeling like you failed Marco?"

"Maybe a little. But I'll get over that, too. I just need some time and your understanding."

The patient look in his soft brown eyes and his gently spoken words made her brave, and Andrea decided to voice her one hope. "Cal, maybe you should give up firefigh—"

He quickly covered her lips with two fingers. "Shh, don't even think it." He chuckled. "Really,

I'm going to be okay. Like I said before, it's just part of the job."

"But, Cal, if you can't—"

Suddenly, he reached up and pulled her head down to his, covering her mouth with his own. He quickly kissed her once, just a soft peck as if exploring for her response, and it came quickly when she returned the kiss, but with more conviction.

Looking into her eyes, his full lips spread in a slow smile before his eyes closed and he kissed her again, this time with all the precision and finesse that Andrea had come to expect. Slowly, he shifted their bodies, bearing her back down into the bedding.

Andrea felt his warm, calloused hands on each of her thighs as he worked his way beneath the thin silk teddy she wore. She gave a sharp gasp, feeling his rising bulge against her thigh.

She moaned softly, feeling his hot breath on her neck and then his warm tongue as he nibbled and licked his way down her neck headed straight for her exposed cleavage.

Unable to hold back any longer, Andrea reached out, taking his head between her hands, needing to kiss him again. She needed the familiar taste of his tongue in her mouth and of their own will, her legs fell open.

Cal knew an invitation when one was extended. He lifted himself up to remove his pajama pants and Andrea immediately sat up to help work them down his hips. He chuckled at her anxiousness, and placed his hands over her trembling ones. Leaning forward, he whispered in her ear.

"If you don't slow down, this is going to be over before it begins."

Ignoring his words, Andrea pressed her hungry mouth against his rock hard midsection, working her way up his warm, muscular chest and continued pushing the offensive pants down his legs. She desperately needed to get them off of him.

Lifting her arms, she waited impatiently for him to unsnap the teddy and pull it over her head. And then her hands were all over him again.

"You're so beautiful," she whined, feeling the ripple of muscles under almost every inch of skin she touched.

Cal gently pushed her back down onto the bed. "No, baby, you are the beautiful one." Coming over her, Cal braced himself on his elbows, as his penis sought her entrance. He struggled to control his breathing, to slow himself down, but it was hard when her warm, wet opening was reaching for him, trying desperately to draw him inside her body.

Andrea felt her heart beating like crazy when the tip of his penis entered her. She parted her legs as wide as possible, wanting nothing more than for him to drive deep inside of her...when the telephone rang making both of them jump in surprise.

Ignoring it, she reached up and grabbed his hips, trying to pull him inside her before it was too late. She had a pretty good idea of who was calling. Whenever his cell phone was turned off, *they* called her house. Just one more reason to despise the Detroit Fire Department.

"Hurry, baby, I need you so bad," she cried, feeling Cal hesitate.

He looked down into her needy eyes, farther down to where their bodies were almost joined, his erection standing at full tilt, then, cursing under his breath, he rolled away from her to answer the phone.

Andrea reacted without thought, slamming her fist against the pillow. "But you're off duty!" She knew she sounded like a spoiled child, but she couldn't help it.

"I'm the chief now, Andrea. I have to be available at all times." He picked up the cordless phone from its base. "Hello?"

His eyes widened and his head swung around to Andrea. Sensing something was terribly wrong, Andrea sat up in the bed as Cal continued the conversation.

"Hello, Mrs. Chenault. Uh, yes, she's here. Um, just one moment." He covered the mouthpiece on the receiver. "I'm sorry, baby. What the hell is your mother doing calling here at two in the morning?" he whispered nervously.

Andrea subconsciously glanced at the clock as if to mentally confirm the time. There was only one reason her mother would be calling at that hour.

Taking a deep, fortifying breath, she accepted the phone. "Hi, Mom."

"Andrea, I'm down at Detroit Receiving Hospital." Margaret Chenault's naturally soft voice was fainter than usual, and Andrea struggled to hear her. "I'm sorry to bother you like this, but do you think you can come get me?"

She was already scooting to the edge of the bed. There was no reason to ask why her mother was in the emergency room at two o'clock in the morning, she already knew.

"I'll be right there." A few seconds later, she hung up the phone and studiously avoided Cal's eyes. She went to the dresser and pulled out a pair of jeans and a sweatshirt.

Cal sat on the side of the bed watching her in silence. The amorous mood had completely dissipated.

Finally, when it became obvious Andrea was not going to volunteer any information, he asked the question, already knowing the answer. "He hit her again, didn't he?"

Andrea was fully dressed and slipping her feet into a pair of sandals. "Yes." She spoke barely above a whisper.

Instantly Cal was behind her protectively wrapping her in his arms, as if he could physically shield her from the pain. He asked another question that he already knew the answer to. "Can I come with you?"

Andrea dropped her head, and whispered, "No."

"Why won't you let me take care of him? Trust me, after I got through with him, he wouldn't be hitting anybody." He spoke with complete conviction, and Andrea believed him, which was why she refused his help.

"He's still my father, Cal."

Cal rested his chin on the top of her head. "Why you feel any loyalty to him is beyond me. But just so we understand each other, Andrea. If he ever lays a finger on you…all bets are off."

She reached up and covered the strong arms that circled her body, savoring the feeling of warmth and love she knew she would need to get through the night. "Like I told you before, he's never hit me. Just her…always her."

"Why won't she leave him?" he whispered in frustration.

Andrea's mind was racing with images from her childhood and well into her adult years. So many memories, most of them not good. "When I have an answer to that question, I'll tell you."

Chapter 4

Three women filed into the spa for their monthly standing reservation. Even in the blue funk that Andrea had been experiencing lately, she couldn't help but get excited about Spa Day.

As soon as they were through the door, the young lady at the counter smiled and greeted them. "Hello, ladies, your suite is ready. Just go on in and Zack will be right with you."

Andrea followed Marty, who followed Dina through the frosted glass doors and into the long corridor that led to the client's suites, ignoring the menacing stares of the walk-in clients who'd been waiting hours to get an appointment with the best masseur in Detroit.

The three were settled quickly into their suite by the spa staff. Their clothes had been traded for incredible soft terry robes. Each pair of tired, aching feet was luxuriating in a small whirlpool tub. They sat sipping on the fruity flavored protein drinks they'd been given to pass the time.

Although they had an appointment, they already knew they would be forced to wait, as well, but it was by choice. The spa employed eight masseurs, but unfortunately there was only one Zack, and everyone wanted him.

Spa Day usually took up all of Andrea's monthly splurge money, but by the time Zack got through kneading and pounding her overworked muscles, somehow she just didn't care.

Once they were well relaxed, and halfway through their protein shakes, they picked up the conversation that had started in the car.

"It's perfectly normal to be nervous, Andrea," Marty said. "You are about to get married—that's a huge commitment."

Andrea shook her head in confusion. "It's more than just that."

Marty just quirked an eyebrow at her friend. "You love him, right? Nothing else should matter."

"You don't understand, Marty," Dina said. "You're one of them—when the bell rings you're on the truck, adrenaline pumping and ready for action. But those of us left behind just waiting and praying, it's different for us. I bet Cavanaugh understands."

"Cavanaugh is completely supportive of my career," she lied, and the other two women just stared at her. Marty stared back, but was unable to keep a straight face. Soon all three women were laughing so loudly the receptionist in the lobby turned her head at the curious noise.

"Okay, okay, maybe he's not *completely* supportive, but he understands this is something I have to do." She pointed a thin finger at Andrea. "And this is something Cal has to do. If you love him, you have to support him."

Andrea had only recently expressed her concerns to her girlfriends, so torn as to what course of action she should take, she felt she could use some unbiased advice. The problem was that neither of her two closest friends was unbiased.

Marty, who was herself a firefighter, saw things only from the point of view of a firefighter, and Dina, Dwight's wife of eight years, a seasoned firefighter's spouse, had nothing but dire warnings regarding the years ahead and often came just short of saying *get-out-while-you-can.*

It may all be a moot point anyway, Andrea thought, but kept her mouth sealed. These women were like the sisters she never had, but she couldn't even confide in them about the nightmares Cal had been having. She knew if Cal found out she was spreading his business around, he would see it as nothing less than a betrayal. And of course, he would find out, considering Dina couldn't keep a secret if you gave it to her under lock and key.

"I don't know. It's just some days, I don't know if I'm cut out to be a fireman's wife."

"So, what are you saying? You're going to call off the wedding?"

Andrea toyed with her ring. "I don't know what I'm going to do."

"Well, you better be sure before you go breaking Cal's heart!" Marty snapped defensively.

"Marty!" Dina scowled. "It's not like the girl don't have enough guilt without your two cents. Look, Andrea, I understand what you are going through. I went through something similar back when Dwight and I first got married."

"How did you get through it?"

"What are you talking about—get through? I'm still *going* through!" Dina half chuckled. "And I will be until he retires." Dina reached across and touched Andrea's hand. "Andrea… any sane woman is going to have doubts about marrying a man who wants to run into burning buildings. But despite all my fears and woes, I understood then and now that there is no one I want to grow old with more than Dwight."

Andrea turned and looked at her. "And what if you never get a chance to grow old together?"

"That is the chance you take. If you can't handle that you need to let him go now."

"Look, you could marry a businessman and he gets hit crossing the street one day. Nothing in life is guaranteed." Marty leaned forward to stress her point. "Andrea, I don't think you realize that what we do is not just a job, it's a *calling*. Honestly, I don't know if I could do anything else, and I think I can say the same for Cal. This is in our blood—it's a part of who we are. Can you understand that?"

"Yes, this is why I haven't asked him to give

it up for me." Andrea, could not resist the urge to offer up a bread crumb of information, to feel them out about the fire that Cal wouldn't talk about. "But what if…there were circumstances beyond his control? Something that forced him to give it up?"

Dina and Marty gave each other a knowing glance. "Are we talking about what happened in the Hadley building downtown about a month ago?" Dina asked.

Andrea struggled to close her mouth which had fallen open at how quickly they'd figured out her small clue.

What Andrea had not realized yet was that the members of Firehouse Fifteen were as close as a real family. And like any loving family, they tended to stay in each other's business.

Everyone had noticed the subtle changes in Cal since the fall. It had been the talk in every home over the past few weeks. Primarily, because it was the closest that their team had come to losing one of their own in almost twenty years.

"No, no, nothing specific." She shuddered nervously and Dina and Marty exchanged another glance.

"I was just saying, if there was some—oh,

never mind!" Andrea slammed her head back
against the leather chair and let out a large frustrated breath.

Marty studied her troubled face. She'd met
Andrea the previous year when she'd been
brought in for smoke inhalation and placed on
Andrea's ward. She'd liked the nurse right off
and as they became friends, Marty soon discovered Andrea was not only kind and fun to be
with, she was a lousy liar. In Marty's estimation,
those were all the traits of a good friend.

"By the way, I forgot to mention this earlier,"
Dina started in an attempt to change the subject.
"Did you ladies know that Dwight is supposedly
planning a surprise bachelor party for Cal?"

Marty quirked an eyebrow. "So what?"

Dina's eyes widened in amazement. "So
what? Do you know what they do at those par-
ties? Bring in a bunch of booty-shaking hoochies
and get all liquored up!"

Marty settled back in her chair. "Come on,
Dina, lighten up. It's just the last hurrah before
he gives up the bachelor life forever. Cut the guys
some slack." She glanced at Andrea. "Unless,
you have a problem with it?"

Andrea, who'd been lost in thought, realized

they were both staring at her. "What? Oh, doesn't make me any difference," she said with the shrug of her shoulders.

"Fine, suit yourself." Dina twisted her mouth, realizing she would get no support for her moral outrage. "I'm just glad Dwight didn't feel the need for such low, debasing entertainment."

Marty snickered. "At least, none that he let you know about."

"What are you saying—Dwight had a bachelor party without my knowledge?"

Before Marty could respond, an energetic man bounced into the room. "Hello, ladies!"

Andrea smiled in greeting, remembering the first time she'd seen Zack Aquinas, one of the most sought-after men in Detroit. Spa Day had originally been Dina's idea, and from the way she had described the masseur, Andrea had expected him to look like something off the cover of a romance novel: tall, lean and beyond-belief gorgeous, when in truth he was a small, round man with a cherubic face. Not physically unpleasant, but certainly nothing worth throwing your panties at.

Andrea had almost laughed out loud at the comical image, until she stretched out on his

table and experienced the magic for herself. The
man's hand were like living silk, and as if guided
by some inner knowledge he had worked her taut
shoulders and lower back until she felt like a ball
of pliable rubber. After that first session, Andrea
slept better than she had in years. It only took one
more session to turn her into a Zack groupie.

As they followed him to the tables, Andrea
found that she was relieved that Zack had arrived
when he did. She was starting to regret consulting
her opinionated friends; with their conflicting
opinions, they'd only left her more confused than
she already was. Not that any of it mattered anyway.
In the end the decision would have to be hers.

Across town at the firehouse, Cal was finishing up his daily sixty-minute workout by adding
another twenty-pound weight to each end of the
pole and securing it in place with the locks. He
glanced back at the doorway beside one of the
gym equipment cabinets.

"Something on your mind, Jeff?" he asked,
before shaking the light sprinkling of dust from
his hands and positioning himself on the bench
to lift the one hundred and fifty pounds over his
chest.

Jeff Collins froze in his hiding place behind the large metal cabinet. He glanced at the opposite wall, noticing for the first time the large mirror that revealed his presence. He'd assumed Cal was too involved in his workout routine to notice anything.

Assuming what he hoped was a casual posture, he stepped out into the open. "No, not really."

Cal shrugged and lifted the bar. Pushing up with fairly little exertion, he completed ten repetitions before replacing the bar. Cal glanced at his friend. "Hey, man, I know that the promotion thing—I mean, I don't want there to be any hard feelings."

Jeff stood over the bench. "No hard feelings."

Cal glanced at him. Something in Jeff's voice said otherwise.

"I'm just here to do a job."

Cal sat up, and grabbing a towel off a nearby bench, he wiped his face. "Glad to hear that." Cal still felt the need to give a warning. He slung the towel around his neck and stood. "After all, a firehouse is no place for a hot dog."

"What are you trying to say to me, Cal?"

Cal shrugged. "Nothing a veteran like you doesn't already know." With that statement, he turned and walked out of the gym.

Jeff's head swung around and his eyes followed Cal until he disappeared around the corner. Only then did he allow his face to relax. The ugly sneer that seemed to be a part of his permanent expression reappeared, along with the cool, dead look in his hard, dark eyes.

Cal walked along the hall toward his office, mentally replaying the conversation. There was something not quite right about Jeff Collins since he'd been promoted. It was obvious the man was feeling the sting of being overlooked for a promotion he thought was guaranteed.

It made no sense, considering Cal was the one to recommend him for the promotion. But ultimately, the decision had been in the hands of the council and they had chosen Cal. But there was something in Jeff's eyes...the intense hatred he'd seen in the man's eyes seemed excessive for such a minor offense. Maybe the guy had mental problems that were not listed in his departmental record.

Cal rubbed his chin thoughtfully—wouldn't be the first time an unstable person had gotten by the shrink at the academy. But with something like that only time could tell. For now, Cal thought, he would just keep an eye on Jeff, just in case.

He was almost back to his office when he was approached by Noel, their district chief fire marshal. "Hey, Cal, got a minute?"

Cal opened the door and motioned his friend inside. "Sure, what'cha need?"

Noel handed him a folder. "Need you to sign off on the Hadley building."

As the fire team responding to the call, Cal was obligated to verify the information in the report for any potential lawsuits. "Did anything seem strange about that fire?" Cal asked Noel as he scribbled his name across the forms, trying to sound as nonchalant as possible.

"Do you mean about the fire or finding the kid inside?"

Cal frowned. "When I think about it, finding Marco there should not have been that much of a surprise. I've been aware for some time that kids like to hang out in there. Everyone from the little bitty ones to the teens seems to be able to find a use for that building. But, no, I was asking about the cause of the fire itself."

"Completely accidental." He motioned to the folder. "Read for yourself."

"Yeah, I did. Just was wondering if there was anything outside of the report."

Noel tilted his head to study his friend. "What's this all about, Cal?"

Cal quickly shook his head trying to deflect his friend's suspicions. He was hoping he would feel the man out subtly, but Noel was no fool. "Nothing, just wondering. Here you go." He smiled and handed back the folder.

"Sure?"

Cal stood and patted him on the back. "You know how I am, man."

Noel smiled. "I forgot how anal you get about stuff. But don't worry, this was classic by-the-book accidental burning. It seemed to be started by some kind of small explosive, like a fire-cracker. Probably kids, but since I can't prove it there is nothing that can be done about it."

Cal saw his friend out before returning to the work on his desk, but unable to concentrate he soon found himself standing at the window looking out over the busy avenue below.

When the dizziness and nightmares had started Cal had brushed them off as being the aftereffects of the fire. But now, several weeks later, he was still experiencing all the same symptoms, but with even more frequency.

He'd hoped there would be some explanation

for all of it when he saw Noel's write-ups, but he'd known almost the instant he looked at it that it was just a standard investigation report.

No insidious chemicals were used, no mind-altering drugs were released in the atmosphere. And Cal was forced to accept that whatever was going on with him…was just him.

Chapter 5

Two hours after her massage, Andrea pulled into her parents' driveway. She could feel the effects of Zack's hard work beginning to wear off. The tension was already returning to her neck and shoulders.

She glanced at her watch to check the time, and nodded in satisfaction. Her father would not be home from work for another two hours. She planned to be long gone before then.

She grabbed the bag from the local pharmacy off the passenger seat, hopped out of her little Mercury Mariner and headed for the side door. She walked along the red brick path that led a windy trail through the beautifully manicured garden.

She looked over the fence that ran the length of the house at the neatly cut lawn and tried to ignore the empty doghouse that sat against the back gate. Her eyes flashed to it anyway. No dog had lived in it for almost twelve years, but Andrea knew her father left it there as a reminder to her, a silent warning not to interfere in his business.

When Andrea was preparing to leave home for college, she found her days and nights plagued with concern for her mother. Not that her presence in the house had ever hindered Andrew Chenault in any way, but she felt that she'd always served as some kind of buffer.

She kept having daydreams of coming home for a holiday break and discovering her mother's lifeless body. A month before she was to leave for school, an idea came to her, and the fact that it was right before Mother's Day made it perfect. Andrea had asked her father if it would be all right to give her mother a dog for Mother's Day.

The fact that they both knew what an animal lover her mother was, her father had agreed. Andrea knew her father expected her to bring home a five-pound purse dog that would bounce and yelp and do little else. She would never forget the way his eyes narrowed on her face when she came through the door with a fully grown, two-hundred-pound female rottweiler.

Even though she had not openly defied him—after all, there had been no agreement on what type of dog she would buy—she knew he felt deceived. As far as Andrea could remember, that was the day he let down the pretense he'd maintained throughout her youth of being a loving father and husband. After that, they became unspoken adversaries.

Of course, the dog had taken to her gentle-natured mother right off, just as Andrea knew she would. Her mother had laughingly named her Buttercup. Andrea had few memories of her mother ever being happier than the day she received her. The dog followed Margaret everywhere, and although she never growled at him, Buttercup watched Andrew with an instinctive wariness.

That last month before she left for school, Andrea believed their home was the most at peace it had ever been and she left with a clear conscience. However, less than two weeks later, her distraught mother called her dormitory, and through the tears and slurred speech conveyed the tale that Buttercup had run away. Andrea never knew if the slurred speech was due to alcohol or a busted lip.

When she came home for the holidays five months later, the doghouse was still sitting against the fence in the backyard.

Andrea confronted her father as to why he hadn't gotten rid of the painful reminder. He'd smiled and said, "Who knows, maybe one day Buttercup will come home."

Despite all the things she'd seen her father do over the course of a lifetime, it wasn't until that moment that she'd begun to hate him.

She knocked lightly on the side door to get her mother's attention. Margaret, standing at the sink, looked up at the noise and smiled. She quickly wiped her hands on her apron and opened the screen door.

"Hi, sweetheart." She swung the door open and stepped back out of the way. Andrea entered and hugged her mother. She handed off the bag, and began with her usual statement. "I can't stay long."

"I know," Margaret muttered, "but hopefully long enough to share a cup of coffee."

Andrea smiled. "Sure, why not?" She glanced

at the table and saw brochures spread out and neatly arranged. "What's this?"

Margaret smiled with a genuine twinkle in her brown eyes. "Your father's taking me on vacation for our anniversary. He told me to pick any place in the world I want to go." She gestured to the pamphlets. "There are so many wonderful places, I can't decide."

Andrea smiled and took an empty seat. *Payoff time,* she thought. Trying to wrap her mind around something she'd accepted years ago.

Her mother at fifty-two was still an incredibly beautiful woman, and always had been. She'd married her college sweetheart thirty years ago, and after two miscarriages, gave birth to their one and only surviving child, a healthy baby girl.

Andrew Chenault had been born into a savings and loan conglomerate, and at the tender age of twenty-five, he'd been given the reins of his family's largest mortgage firm which he'd doubled in size over the past twenty years.

On paper, her parents had the ideal marriage. A beautiful home in an affluent neighborhood; Margaret was active in several different charitable causes, and Andrew was a doting husband in public. They took several vacations a year and their friends envied them.

But then again, Andrea thought, their friends did not live in the house with them. So many times, Andrea had tried to convince her mother to leave her father, but all she ever succeeded in doing was driving a wedge between herself and her mother.

So she stopped trying, and now they both pretended like theirs was a normal family. After being an E.R. nurse for ten years, Andrea had come to realize that in many respects they were a normal family. And crazy as it seemed, despite the occasional late-night trip to the emergency room, her mother seemed satisfied with her life.

"How about a cruise to the Bahamas?" Andrea asked, trying to be supportive.

Margaret laughed. "You do realize it's hurricane season." She shook her head. "No, I was thinking something more exotic." She held up a leaflet with a picture of an ancient ruin on the cover, grinning with all the enthusiasm of a small child, and Andrea found herself unable to help smiling in return.

She took the brochure and read. "A Mayan village in South America?"

"Just think, a civilization older than most of the world, and parts of it are still standing."

Andrea put down the pamphlet. "Whatever makes you happy."

Margaret sat at the table and her eyes flashed slyly over Andrea's face. "Speaking of what makes us happy, would you care to explain why Cal was answering your phone at two o'clock in the morning?"

Andrea quirked her mouth. "Are you looking for a reason other than the obvious?"

"Andrea, I'm surprised at you. I would've thought you'd save yourself for your wedding night."

Andrea's eyes widened at the genuine shock in her mother's voice. *You have got to be kidding me.* "Uh, yeah, well, we decided we didn't want to buy the car without giving it a little test drive."

Margaret's mouth fell open and Andrea couldn't help laughing. It seems she'd offended her mother's delicate senses. "Just how many men have...*test driven* you?"

"Mom! I'm not going to answer that! Geez, what a question!"

"I raised you to be a lady."

"I am a lady!" *A sexually satisfied lady.* "Can

we talk about something else?" Andrea could feel herself beginning to blush. She shook her head—thirty-four and still unable to discuss sex with her mother.

Margaret pursed her lips thoughtfully, and Andrea knew she wanted to continue the interrogation, but instead she hopped up from the table and went to prepare two cups of coffee. "Two sugars and three creams, right?" she called over her shoulder, and Andrea confirmed it.

"Andrea…" Margaret began hesitantly, still facing the coffeepot. "Do you feel…safe with Cal?"

Andrea had been looking through the brochures, but her head came up. "Yes, very safe."

"Are you sure?"

Andrea studied her mother's ramrod straight back and realized that in her entire life, she could not ever remember seeing her mother slouch. "Yes, Mom, I feel safe and protected with Cal."

Andrea had never told her mother about her concerns regarding Cal's line of work. Andrea loved her mother, but there was something in knowing that her mother *wanted* to stay with her father, despite what he did to her, that made it impossible to completely trust her.

Margaret nodded vigorously. "Good, good. It's important to feel safe."

And what about you, Mom? Who's going to make you feel safe? In past conversations, this was where Andrea would've questioned her mother regarding her reasons for staying. This was where she would've begged and pleaded with her to leave. She'd stopped doing that a long time ago.

No more was said about feeling safe. And although Margaret tried to steer the conversation back that way more than once, Andrea kept the line of conversation away from her sex life. The ladies spent the next hour looking through brochures and laughing at the possibilities of visiting each locale.

She was so enjoying herself, Andrea lost track of the time and did not realize how late it was until she heard the sound of her father's Cadillac pulling into the driveway.

She froze in place and gently set the brochure for Bora Bora back on the table. "I'd really better be going." She stood and quickly placed her coffee cup in the sink, then checked the table to make sure she had put nothing else out of place and watched as her mother did the same. Her heart sank. *A lifetime of conditioning,* she thought.

She kissed her mother's cheek, but before she could slip out the side door, her father appeared in the entryway to the kitchen.

He smiled, seeming genuinely pleased to see his daughter. "Well, if it isn't the prodigal daughter." He held his arms opened for a hug, and Andrea resisted, but in the end she went into them, knowing somewhere in the back of her brain, the little girl in her was still looking for the daddy who would push her swing all the way to the top. The daddy who would bring home gifts from every business trip. The daddy who gave the very best belly tickles. Some part of her would always remember him that way.

She hugged him briefly. "Hi, Daddy."

Andrew Chenault took in the kitchen with one sweeping glance, and seemed satisfied with what he found. He glanced at the brochures neatly stacked on the table. "Your mother tell you about our vacation?"

Andrea nodded.

"You know you're welcome to come along."

Andrea forced a smile. "No, thanks, with the wedding less than four months away, I've got a lot of work to do." Andrea knew she could've given a million excuses for not wanting to travel with them, but she always, always chose the one that involved Cal.

Shameful as it was, she knew she used her fiancé like a battle shield. The two men, Cal and her father, had only met once, and had almost come to blows. Andrea knew her father was intimidated by a man that towered over him. Some dark part of her reveled in it.

"I've got to be going."

"Sure you can't stay for dinner? I've missed you." Andrew tilted his head to look at her where she was still cradled in his arm.

Andrea glanced at his face and was surprised to see sincerity in his eyes. "No, I've got to get going." She broke free of his loose hold, hugged her mother, and headed out the back door.

She hurried down the path, hopped in her car and pulled out of the driveway as quickly as possible. Andrea quickly let down her car windows and took in a big gulp of fresh air as the suffocating feeling began to subside.

She picked up her cell phone, and pressed the speed dial button for Cal.

"Hey, baby," Cal answered on the first ring.

"How much longer?" she asked, knowing that he was ending a rotation this evening. She was anxious to see him.

"Not long, just finishing up some paperwork."

"What did you want to do tonight?" she asked, hoping he would not say crash at her place. Andrea was feeling the need to get out and do something.

As if sensing the need, he asked, "How do you feel about carnivals?"

"Carnivals?"

"Yeah, there is one down the street from the firehouse. Wanna go? Maybe I can win you one of those giant pink elephants."

"Ooohh, a giant pink elephant," Andrea purred. "You spoil me."

"I know. Wanna go?"

"Sure, why not?" she said, while trying to stifle a yawn.

"See, that's what I love about you, your *enthusiasm.*"

A few minutes later, when Andrea hung up the phone she was still smiling. In a matter of minutes, Cal had managed to lift the dark cloud that always followed her away from her childhood home.

Sometimes, Andrea felt as if she were a

prisoner who'd been forced to spend an eternity in the darkness, never knowing what it felt like to have the sun on her face. Until Cal came into her life throwing open the shutters, and guiding her into the light of love and laughter. Despite whatever doubts she had about their relationship, Andrea knew that life with Cal meant never having to live in the darkness again.

Chapter 6

"Step right up, folks and try your luck!" The heckler moved back and forth across the grassy area before his exhibit, trying desperately to coerce patrons. It was already past 8:00 p.m. and he'd only had about thirty percent of his typical turnout. The light drizzle of rain that had been falling all day kept a large number of carnival attendees away and in a few very short hours he would have to pack up for the night.

Just then, his eyes fell on the large man and petite woman moving in his direction. He saw his opportunity. So desperate for this score, he stepped outside of his safety zone to cross into the man's path. "How about you, sir? You look like a veritable Hercules. Surely, a mammoth of a man such as yourself can quickly win a prize for your lady."

Cal looked down into the greedy little face of the man who'd practically jumped into his path, and then looked at Andrea, who was presently cradling the four stuffed animals he'd won for her already. "No, thanks." He went to step around the man.

The man gasped in false alarm. "Afraid of a challenge, my good man?" The heckler turned to the crowd of people beginning to gather. "What do you say, folks? Do you think our little exhibit can present a challenge to this friendly giant?"

Cal looked around at the curious faces, and felt his jaw flex. The little man was becoming a nuisance, not to mention drawing unwanted attention. He could've easily swatted him out of his way and kept walking. But now, Andrea was looking up at him with that pleading expression that always got to him.

"What?"

Her eyes twinkled as she gingerly pointed to something on the wall of the booth.

Cal's eyes followed her finger. "Aww, hell," Cal sighed in defeat when his eyes fell on the big, pink elephant tacked against the back booth wall.

"Fine." He threw up his hands in surrender. "What do I have to do?"

The heckler gave a greasy smile, sensing victory. "Well, just step up to the red dot and I'll tell you!" he continued in a loud manner. Hoping the big man would draw enough interest to hook other suckers.

He handed Cal a large, oversized mallet. "At the sound of the bell, just hammer the ball as hard as you can, and send the red light zooming to the top!" Cal looked over his shoulder at Andrea who, so sure of his success, was eyeing the stuffed trophy as if it were already hers.

The heckler stepped back and discreetly eyed the crowd. There were several people gathered around now. Soon, they would see the big man fail in his attempt to send the light all the way to the top, and curiosity and ego would force many of them to take their own swing at it. This little distraction worked nine out of ten times.

Cal lifted the mallet over his head and swung, hitting the target dead center which created a loud thump. The heckler winced, realizing the man could easily break his contraption. Everyone watched as the red light quickly moved up the narrow tube, only to stop four notches from the top.

Cal frowned in confusion, knowing his own strength too well to believe the meter. "What the…?" He turned his anger on the little man.

The heckler swallowed hard as he looked up into the face of an angry giant. He suddenly remembered why he'd stopped using this tactic. There was always the chance that his bait would turn on him.

"Sorry, sir, but apparently you don't have what it takes." He quickly moved away from Cal's side toward the crowd. "Is there anyone else who thinks he can beat the meter?"

A thin, lanky, white teenager was studying Cal with calculating eyes. "I'll try it."

He stepped forward and Cal handed over the mallet. "The game's rigged, man."

The young man's mouth twisted in sarcasm. "Sure it is."

Cal just shook his head and stepped back. He watched as the guy lifted the mallet and swung with a portion of the force Cal had used.

Everyone's attention was riveted on the red

light as it floated up the narrow tube, no one noticed the small device in the hand of the heckler, or saw when he pushed a button on the device. All they saw was the red light sail right up to the top of the meter.

"What?" Cal turned on the little man once more. "No way! This thing is rigged!"

The teen just smirked at Cal, before going to collect his prize.

Cal grabbed Andrea's hand and quickly moved away. His long legs taking well-spaced strides, forcing her to run along to keep up. "Cal, slow down!"

He continued to charge across the open field, passing by exhibit after exhibit. "We're leaving."

"Why? I was having a good time."

"That stupid game was rigged, Andrea. I don't care what he says! It was rigged."

She pulled back and dug in her heels, and was more surprised than Cal to realize it worked. He'd lost his grip on her hand. Realizing her fingers were slipping through his, he turned in surprise.

"Well, of course it's rigged! But I don't see why we have to leave because of it."

Somewhere in the back of his mind, Cal

realized he was overreacting, but on top of everything else that had been happening lately, getting beat by a rigged game was just too much.

Ever since the fire in that Hadley building, Cal had felt as if his world was spinning out of control and it was taking everything in him to hold it all together.

His team members, who had once thought he was indestructible, now gave him strange, questioning looks when they thought he wasn't watching. Not the least of which, the new guy Jeff, who seemed determined to challenge him at every turn.

And Andrea...he had no idea how Andrea saw him anymore. Being that she was the one who had to wake him up out of his cold sweats whenever they spent the night together, he could only imagine how many notches he'd gone down in her opinion.

Knowing that, how was he supposed to tell her about the *daymares*. He didn't know what else to call a nightmare that could occur at any time. The hallucinations that came out of nowhere, the dizziness he'd recently begun to experience whenever he went up high; his new fear of loose hoses, defective hoses, defective equipment, the firehouse alarm and anything else that went along with being a firefighter.

He felt as if some invisible monster was slowly stealing his manhood, a monster that he could not see, or stop. And the worst fear of all was that if anyone ever realized what was really going on, he could lose everything he'd worked for his whole life. Not only his recent promotion, but his whole career, and…Andrea, as well.

So much pressure had been building up over the past month, and it had all come together in the moment he swung that mallet. Somehow, a small carnival game had come to represent his life, and according to that game, he was weak in both mind and body.

Andrea could see the conflicting emotions swirling in the depths of his eyes. "Don't you get it? He needed for someone like you to lose—not just anyone, someone just like you. What did he call you? A *mammoth* of a man. Then he needed someone like that skinny kid to win. After all, everyone would *expect* you to win, not the other guy. When you didn't, it gave them the impression that maybe they could. It was a scam." Her mouth twisted. "And not a very good one. But people believe what they want to believe."

I knew that, Cal thought looking at her. *I just didn't realize you did.* His heart was filling up with all the things he felt for this woman. All those feelings that still occasionally caught him by surprise.

"I love you." Until that moment, Cal had not realized how much he needed her unwavering faith.

"I love you, too," she said, offhandedly, looking over her shoulder at the concession stand. "Now, can we stay? I'm starving, and there's a foot-long hot dog over there with my name on it."

Cal chuckled and put his arm around her shoulder as they started moving in the direction of the concession stand. *Everything is going to work out okay—the dizziness, the nightmares, all just a thing. It will pass, and everything will be back to normal soon...soon.*

A few weeks later, Cal stood leaning against the side of his desk receiving a token for his heroism. Although Marco had come home from the hospital shortly after he did, Cal had not seen the boy in over a month.

Marco was explaining how his protective mother refused to let him leave the house until now, and how he'd wanted to come sooner.

Looking at the strangely light-colored patch of skin on Marco's brown arm, he understood. It was an instant reminder of how close she'd come to losing him.

"I just wanted you to have this." Marco moved forward and handed over the small object. "You know, for rescuing me."

Cal accepted the decoratively colored rock, flipping it this way and that in earnest examination. "Wow, thanks, man." He hesitated, but then decided it was better to be safe than sorry. "Um, what is it?"

"It's rock art." He pointed to the drawing of a bird. "It's a Thunderbird. It's my favorite rock."

"And you're giving it to me?" Cal couldn't help being touched by the selfless gesture. "I can't accept this, little man. And besides, I could never take as good care of it as you do."

Marco's eyebrows came together in a thin, crinkled line over his eyes. "You don't want it?"

"No! No, that's not what I'm saying. I'm honored—" He waved his hand, realizing the more he talked the more crinkled that line got. "You know what, never mind. I will cherish it. Thanks, little man."

The crinkled line disappeared as a full grin

came across his face. "No problem. I can always make more."

"Listen, I'm glad you came by here today. I've been meaning to talk to you." Cal gently placed the rock on the desk behind him. "I know what you were doing in that old building downtown and it's not cool."

Marco dropped his head in shame. "But I had to, Cal. I couldn't let them think I was chicken."

"What's more important? Being a dead tough guy, or a living chicken?"

Marco smiled, as Cal had hoped. "Look man, no one's asking you to be a coward. But there is no reason to take unnecessary risks."

"You take risks every day." The twelve-year-old argued like a lawyer.

"Yeah, but I don't take stupid risk. When I take risks something important is at stake."

The boy's smile widened. "Like me?" he asked, remembering Cal's heroic rescue.

Cal smiled and lightly punched his arm. "Yeah, like you." He glanced back at his new trophy sitting still on the desk. Up until this afternoon, he'd considered the rescue in that building to be a failure and he was pretty sure everyone else felt that way, as well.

The building had been destroyed, Marco had gotten burned, not to mention whatever craziness was now going on in his head.

But when Marco had walked in with the small package and eyes still filled with hero worship, Cal suddenly realized he'd let his ego get in the way of what was really important. The boy was alive, no one had been seriously injured, they were alive to tell the tale, and at the end of the day that was all that really mattered.

A soft knock on his door, and they both turned to greet the visitor. Andrea came around the edge of the door and stopped short, surprised to see that Cal already had a visitor.

"Andrea, you remember Marco." He stood and put his hands on the boy's shoulders.

The boy smiled. "Hi."

"Nice to see you again, Marco." Her eyes darted around him to the rock on the desk. "Wow, what's this?"

Once again, Marco explained the significance of the stone and Andrea listened with appropriate awe. "How wonderful! Thank you so much, Marco. When we get our new house, I'll make sure this has a special place."

Cal just stood listening. Of course, Andrea

would know how to handle the whole rock thing, he thought. She didn't even try to give it back.

Marco glanced at his watch. "My mom said I had to be back before seven."

"Better get going—don't want to get you in trouble."

The boy threw up a hand, already in motion. "See you later, Cal."

"Thanks for the gift!" Andrea called after him.

"Uh yeah, thanks!" Cal added far too late.

He walked across the room and closed the door, before wrapping Andrea up in a bear hug. "I tell you what, after we're married, I'll let you handle all the diplomatic stuff, okay?"

She wrapped her arms around his neck, enjoying the feeling of floating she experienced whenever he held her off the ground this way. "I think that goes without saying."

"What's that supposed to mean?"

"You tried to give the rock back, didn't you?"

"Well, it just seem like he worked so hard on it, and it meant so much to him, I felt bad."

She laughed and kissed him.

"What brings you here?" he asked. Pulling away from her soft mouth, he settled her back on her feet.

"This." She reached into her purse and held up

three pictures of silverware. Each had been enlarged to give a perfect picture of the intricate designs on the handles. "I'm going to register tomorrow, and this is the only thing we have not agreed on."

"What agreement? You've just been doing whatever you damn well please." He held up his hands at the aggrieved expression that came across her face. "Which is just fine by me. So, why do you want my input now?"

"For that very reason! You haven't helped me with any of the arrangements. I figured the least you could do is pick the silverware!"

He frowned. "Does it matter? I mean, a fork is a fork, right? They all do pretty much the same thing."

She just stared at him, until he began to question his logic. "Right?" he said after a while, believing he had a valid point.

Andrea huffed and shoved her pictures back down into her purse. "I should've known better than this. Never mind." The wedding was now less than two months away, and Andrea was feeling less sure of her course with every day.

It had become apparent to her that nothing short of God would keep Calvin Brown off the engine truck when that alarm sounded. She thought, or hoped rather, that the problems he'd exhibited after the last fire would've kept him grounded. But she was finally beginning to understand what Marty had meant. It wasn't just a job, it was a calling. And Cal was a devoted believer.

She'd thought that maybe if she forced him to become more active in the planning of the wedding, that somehow it would assuage some of her concern. Maybe, if they spent more time together during these crucial times, she could remind herself of all the reasons she could not live without him. But just as she'd originally suspected, the promotion to chief had only meant more time spent away from her, and more chances of him being killed.

As she headed toward the door, Cal cut off her path. "Okay, what did I do this time?"

She shook her head, fearing that if she spoke, he would hear the tears in her voice.

Taking her in his arms, his large hands slid down to cup her bottom in his palms. "Tell you what. When you are ready to go lingerie shopping for the honeymoon, I'll be all over that!" He grinned wickedly, and Andrea could not help but return the smile. He looked so pleased with the prospect.

He placed a gentle kiss on her forehead. "Look, we both knew when I became chief that there would be more responsibility."

But I never wanted you to become chief! she wanted to scream, but knew the words would crush him.

"Just be patient with me, Andrea. Once I get the hang of the job, I'll be able to delegate more, but right now it all falls on me."

"I understand," she lied. She didn't understand any of it, and everything he was saying just reinforced her own point of view.

"Did I tell you about the house in Puerto Rico?" Cal asked, trying to lift her spirits with the generous offer Marty and Cavanaugh had made.

She looked at him curiously. "Cavanaugh offered us the St. John house in Puerto Rico for our honeymoon if we want. Interested?"

Her eyes widened. Cavanaugh, Marty's husband was a wealthy businessman, and his family owned what they called a villa, but in the pictures the thing looked more like a mansion. Marty had told her all about it from the times she'd stayed there with Cavanaugh. "Sure, how nice of them."

"Yeah, I thought so." He relaxed, seeing the light come back into her eyes. "I'll let him know we want to do it, but you have to give me some specific dates."

She frowned. "Don't you remember the dates we chose for the honeymoon?"

Uh-oh. "Um, of course I do." He moved around the desk. "It's right here in my planner." He quickly flipped through the pages, but could not find it. When he finally looked up again, Andrea was gone.

Cal quirked an eyebrow. Why was she acting so strange lately? Cal had noticed that everything he said to her lately seemed to get taken out of context.

Andrea was storming toward the steps when she saw Dina coming from the opposite direction with a large basket of clothes.

Although the firehouse had two sets of washers and dryers for the guys, Dina always picked up Dwight's laundry and replaced it with clean clothes. It was the unanimous opinion of all the firehouse wives and girlfriends that Dina was setting a bad example.

Andrea paused and waited for her friend. "Hey, girl, see you're here taking care of that big baby."

"Well, what can I say? I created the monster." Dina laughed. "What are you doing here?"

"I came to ask Cal about silverware patterns."

Dina burst into a full body laugh, then it suddenly stopped. "Oh…you're serious."

"His reaction wasn't much better," she confessed.

Seeing the very real concern on her face, Dina leaned against the wall. "Still struggling with that decision?"

"Yes."

Dina glanced back over her shoulder. "Well, you better make up your mind fast, girlfriend. Invitations are going to be going out soon."

"Don't remind me. Where's Marty?"

"On her way here. She starts her new rotation tonight."

"Oh." Andrea sighed, realizing they did not have another Spa Day scheduled for weeks.

"Well, I better get going." Dina leaned forward and whispered, "By the way, don't worry about that little party they were planning to throw for Cal. I've taken care of everything." With a wicked snicker, she hurried down the hall, leaving Andrea standing alone and wondering what the heck she was talking about.

Deciding it was just the rattling of an exhausted woman, she shook it off and went down the stairs. As she rounded the corner, Jeff appeared in front of her out of nowhere.

"Hey, sexy, what's up?"

Andrea frowned slightly at the man's familiar greeting. He hadn't said more than two words in the almost two months he'd been there, and now suddenly it's *Hey, sexy, what's up?*

"Hi…Jeff, right?" She put it in the form of a question to remind him that they did not know each other that well.

He ignored the warning and edged closer. "Funny running into you this way."

Feeling suddenly uncomfortable, Andrea pushed her way around him. "Not really, I'm here all the time—to see Cal—my *fiancé*." She stressed the word, noting for the first time the lecherous look in his eyes. "You remember him, don't you? Your boss."

That did it. His expression snapped to one of anger, and his beady eyes narrowed on her face. "Ain't got to get all defensive. Can't a man just say hello?"

She stared at him for a second, then turned and walked away. Halfway to her car, Andrea decided she would not say anything to Cal about the incident. Knowing Cal, he would hurt the man, and despite his strange behavior she did not want that on her conscience. But in the future, she would definitely avoid him.

Chapter 7

Jeff stood, watching her leave. *Stuck-up bitch*. Up until that moment, Jeff had not decided if Andrea was disposable or not. Now, he knew she most certainly was. He would use her and toss her out without hesitation if it got him closer to his goal.

All he'd said was "hello sexy"—most women would think that was a compliment. And it was not like he was really interested in her—he'd just panicked when he heard someone coming down the back stairs. No one ever used those stairs, which was why he thought he would be left alone for a time.

Brushing off the whole incident, he returned to the task at hand. He stood staring at the hoses on the back of the truck, trying to decide just how badly he wanted to hurt Cal's reputation. Bad enough to tamper with the equipment?

He fingered the heavy hose. If he did what he was considering, he could put the whole team in jeopardy. Cal had seemed to become obsessed with the equipment lately, which is how Jeff had come up with the idea in the first place.

If the equipment was found to be faulty, Cal would be the one held responsible. There would be an investigation, but where would that lead? Jeff frowned in thought. Everyone in the house would vouch for him. No, he decided, tampering with the equipment was not the way.

A small red container caught his eyes and he saw a bottle of accelerant sitting off to the side. It was used for the rare occasion when they had to start a smaller fire to contain a larger one. It was small enough that it would never be missed. But what would he use it for?

Just then, he heard a sports car pull into the lot. He swore under his breath and, taking them two at a time, he quickly went up the back stairs, forgetting he still had the accelerant container tucked in his arm. All that was on his mind was not being seen alone near the truck…just in case he decided to change his mind about sabotaging the equipment later.

Marty sat beside her husband, Cavanaugh, in his small sports car as he pulled into the firehouse lot to drop her off for her latest rotation. Instead of hopping out of the car right away in her usual fashion, she waited patiently for him to speak. Something was on his mind, but Cavanaugh was the type of man who only spoke when he was ready and not a minute before.

"Four more nights without you by my side," he finally said. "I'm beginning to dread these rotations."

So, that was it, she thought. "The time will go fast," she said softly.

He leaned over and kissed her cheek. "No, it won't."

Not knowing how to console him, Marty opened the door and prepared to leave when she felt his hand on her shoulder. "Marty, when are we going to get started on our future?"

She shifted her body on the seat to face him. "What do you mean?"

"I mean kids. When are we going to consider starting a family?"

Marty frowned realizing where this conversation was going. "Certainly not now, if that's what you're getting at."

"Why not?"

"Why not? Well, for one, we've only been married for a year. I don't know about you, but I would like a little more time as a couple before we add children to the equation. Secondly, have you forgotten I'm a firefighter?"

"No," he growled. "I can never forget that."

She tilted her head to the side, wondering if she'd imagined the subtle anger in his voice, but continued to make her point. "Sorry, but they don't make turnout gear in maternity wear."

"You think I don't realize that?"

There was no mistaking the anger this time. "What's this about?"

His jaw flexed with tension. "Nothing. Go on, you're going to be late signing in."

She took his hand between hers.

He continued to stare straight ahead, only the slight flexing of his jawbone revealed his conflicting emotions.

"Is this about the fire last week?"

"It's about the fire last week, the fire the week before. The fire next week, and the week after. It's about every time that firehouse alarm sounds."

"Cavanaugh, you knew what I did when we met."

"Forget I brought it up." His coal-black eyes shot her a darting glance. "I love you, Marty. Sometimes, I don't think you know how much."

"I know."

"I don't know what I would do without you."

She leaned across the seat and kissed his cheek. "I plan to have a long and fruitful life with you. In ten years or so, we'll have a house full of kids. Just not now, not today."

A few seconds later, Marty stood in the entrance of the firehouse and waved as Cavanaugh drove away. She only hoped she'd been able to reassure him.

Cal peered out his office window when he heard Cavanaugh's BMW pulling in. He went to stand at the top of the stairs to greet Marty, and stopped short to see Jeff coming up the stairs with an accelerant can under his arm.

"What are you doing with that?" Cal's cinnamon-brown eyes narrowed to slits.

Jeff nearly fell back down the stairs startled by the shadow that was suddenly standing over him. He quickly regained his composure. "Found it sitting in the middle of the floor downstairs. Just putting it back where it belongs."

"It belongs downstairs."

Jeff feigned surprise. "Oh? I could've sworn I saw a cabinet up here somewhere with all the accelerants in it."

Cal studied the man intensely. He was lying. "No, the cabinet for the accelerants is downstairs."

"Okay, thanks." He turned and hurried back down the stairs almost knocking Marty over in the process.

"Hey! Watch it," she snapped, regaining her balance on the metal, spiral staircase. Once the man was out of sight, she turned to look at Cal at the top of the stairs. He was still staring at the last place he'd seen Jeff. "What's going on?"

Cal shook his head. "Don't know. Does anything strike you odd about that guy?"

Her mouth twisted in a smirk. "Only everything."

So, Cal thought, it wasn't just him. He resolved right there to ask his other team members what their take on Jeff Collins was. He could not

risk a weak link in his strong chain. He was beginning to wonder if he'd made a bad decision
in accepting him as part of his team.

At first, Cal had believed he was just a loner
who could slowly be won over, and made to feel
accepted. But now, after the incident in the
weight room, he was reconsidering. Something
in Jeff's eyes revealed his nature. And from what
Cal could see it was not good. The man was more
than a loner, he was trouble.

"What's up?" Marty asked, seeing the
thoughtful expression on his face.

"Nothing," he said, watching Marty sling her
knapsack over her shoulder and climb the re-
maining stairs. Cal decided to keep his suspicions to himself for now. After all, what did he
have to go on? A feeling?

No, he would wait, and give Jeff a chance to
fit in. Maybe with encouragement and time, he
would change his feelings.

As she came to a halt beside him, Marty
reached over and touched his arm. "Are you
okay? I mean, since the Hadley building you've
been acting a little weird."

"It shook me a little, but I'm fine now," he said

the words, at the same time trying to make himself believe them.

Marty started to move, but then paused. "Andrea is worried about you."

His eyes flashed to Marty's, wondering just how much Andrea said to her, but he was instantly relieved. One look in her eyes told him she knew nothing of the nightmares.

"I know." He smiled. "Really, I'm good."

His friend looked at him for a long time, before deciding to accept his words. She nodded and walked away. A few seconds later Cal heard the guys greeting her in the other room.

As he headed back to his office, he replayed the incident that had occurred at her place the night before. Andrea had pleaded with him to talk to her about his nightmares. He could still see the love and compassion shining in her eyes.

But instead, he put on his clothes and left. He remembered exactly how she looked sitting so lonesome on the big, empty bed. He sometimes wondered if she wouldn't be better off without him. Driving home, for one brief, terrifying moment, he imagined what his life would've been like if he walked away from her, out of her life forever. The image was terrifying. The bleak, lonely existence that waited beyond was too horrible to imagine. So, he found himself in an impossible position. Too weak to love her, the way she deserved to be loved, and too weak to let her go.

And he'd almost caved. He'd wanted to cross the room and take her into his arms, tell her again how much he loved her, how lucky he was that she loved him. He wanted to tell her that he would love and honor her the rest of her days, and treat her like the princess she was. But he couldn't because he knew she deserved better than a half-crazed fireman. So, when she reached out to him, he'd tucked his tail and run. But what choice did he have?

How was he supposed to tell her that the nightmare she'd awaken him from involved her? That many times, over the past few nights, the person he'd seen falling into the great abyss had not been himself, but the one he loved most. Somehow the demon in his mind knew just how to terrify him. Not with the threat of his own death, but with that of Andrea's.

Suddenly, the shrill and familiar sound of the alarm interrupted his contemplation, and once again the firehouse erupted in activity. By the time he got into gear and hurried down the stairs, most of the team was already on the truck. The horn blew twice in warning to pedestrians, and the truck began moving forward, just as Cal was pulled aboard by Tommy.

Cal spotted the shadowy outline of what he believed was a human body at the top of the stairwell. The ear-piercing scream that came shortly after confirmed that the person was still alive. He took two steps at a time, until he reached the first landing. He turned, stepped over a pile of debris and stopped dead cold.

The second flight of stairs had burned away, leaving an eight foot gap between where he stood and his victim. Without thought, he looked down into the hideous cavity and immediately regretted it as the whole world took on the sickening, swirling effect. He braced himself against the wall, and closed his eyes. Sometimes taking several deep breaths helped, but not this time.

When he opened his eyes again, it was even worse. Everything had taken on a kaleidoscopic appearance. Images running one into the other, and he was no longer certain of exactly where his victim lay. No more sure than he was of where he was standing.

The person lying at the top of the stairs screamed again, calling for help.

Cal turned his head trying to pinpoint the person; he knew they couldn't last much longer. The flames were closing in on their location. With material to feed on, the fire moved with a swiftness that always amazed him.

He tried to stand, and fell back against the wall. His legs felt like melting rubber beneath his body. Suddenly, it felt as if his oxygen had been cut off. He found it almost impossible to breath. He took big, gulping, mouthfuls of air and still felt as if he were suffocating.

"Cal! What are you doing?"

Cal felt another firefighter push past him, and he went to grab them. Apparently, they did not see the hole in the staircase. "No wait!" he called out beneath his mask, but it was too late. The person had disappeared into the flames.

Seconds later, they reappeared with the victim tossed over a shoulder, and Cal got his first clear look at the face beneath the mask. It was Dwight.

"Come on! Let's get out of here!" Dwight pushed back past Cal once again, hurrying toward the direction of the exit. It only took a moment to realize Cal was not following.

Cal stood looking down at the perfectly secure staircase; the one that he'd thought had burned away. They were all there, not a single stair touched by flames. That's how Dwight had reached the victim; he'd simply climbed the stairs. Stairs that, until a moment ago, Cal could not see.

"Cal! Let's go!" Dwight called again.

Cal looked up at his friend in dumbfounded silence, as the flames continued to lap at them on all sides.

Someone grabbed his arm, and dragged him forward. Almost to the exit, he realized there was a whole group of them. Where had they all come from? Where had those mysterious stairs come from? Or had they been there all along?

As they exited the family home, Cal felt himself being pushed aside as the medical techs took over the scene. He stumbled over to the truck, and leaned his heavy weight against it. His head was still spinning, but not as much as inside the house.

He could finally take in the scene with some accuracy. Now he saw the family lying on the grass, all alive and choking on smoke. A man, a teenage girl, and now the victim Dwight was adding, a woman.

Cal felt his insides twist into tight knots as he watched the victim he'd been unable to reach, the woman at the top of the stairs he could not see, struggle to breathe. The sharp shooting pain in his chest caused him to double over.

"You all right, Cal?"

Cal looked up into the smug face of Jeff. Things were still somewhat disoriented. What was the man saying?

Jeff leaned forward closed to Cal's ear. "Next time, I might not be there to save your ass."

Cal heard the tone of superiority that underlined the statement. So, it had been Jeff who'd pulled him through the blaze. He glanced past Jeff, and saw most of his team standing off to the side in heavy discussions amongst themselves. Every once in a while someone would glance in his direction, and he knew his behavior inside the building was the main topic.

What was he supposed to tell them? That he'd not rescued the woman because he could not see the stairs leading up to her? They'd never believe it, since they all saw the same thing. Cal leaning against a wall in helplessness, while Dwight was forced to rescue the victim.

Jeff was still bragging about his quick thinking and how fast everything had happened. Cal had tuned him out. He was more concerned with what his friends were saying. He knew what they were thinking. Hell, he'd had the same thoughts himself. Had he lost his edge?

Almost two hours later, back at the firehouse, Cal was sitting in front of the television flipping through the channels when he decided he'd had enough. All afternoon he'd been forced to listen as Jeff went on and on about pulling him through the fire. Cal had stopped being grateful two hours ago. Now, he just wanted to shut him up.

Cal put down the remote and headed in the direction of the kitchen. As he came through the door, Jeff was droning on about his *lightninglike* reflexes.

He leaned against the door frame, noting that the only audience Jeff had was KC, the youngest member of their team. Not that KC was listening. His attention seemed to be fully focused on the sandwich he was making.

"Anyway, had I not been there," Jeff continued, "who knows what would've happened."

Cal stood and came forward into the room. "All right Jeff, enough is enough. I think you are making too big a deal out of this."

Jeff's eyes narrowed and a wide smile came over his face. Cal thought the overall effect reminded him of a snake.

"Face it, Cal. You don't belong here. You just can't cut it anymore."

Cal flinched slightly. The cutting remarks caused KC to pause momentarily, then he scooped up the plate with his completed sandwich and quickly left the room. Cal did not miss the fact that the young man would not even make eye contact.

He took a deep breath trying to hold back the urge to break Jeff Collins in half over his knee. "There is no reason for all that, man."

Jeff stood from where he'd been sitting at the table, and came toward the door. "Tell you what. Next time the alarm sounds, why don't you stay behind and let the *real men* take the call." He touched his chin. "And you can bake us some cookies while you're waiting."

Cal reacted before his brain had a chance to catch up with his fist, and he found himself standing over Jeff's prone body. He looked down

at the moaning man not completely regretting
his action, then without another word he turned
and walked away.

Chapter 8

"With all due respect, sir, I haven't lost my edge." Cal fought with every strand of willpower he could muster to keep control of his temper. Since his altercation with Jeff, he seemed to have lost complete control of it. He'd been snapping and snarling at everyone over the past week, so he wasn't completely surprised to look up and find his boss standing in his doorway.

"No one is saying you have, Cal." Captain Mark McKinley, a large burly white man commonly known as Mack, stood leaning back against Cal's office desk, his thick arms crossed over his chest, watching the emotions play across Cal's expressive face.

"This suspension is department policy, you know that. Whatever happened in that house has to be addressed. There has to be a formal hearing, and there is not a damn thing I can do about it." He stood away from the desk. "Look, don't make this any harder than it has to be."

Cal tightened his lips in a thin line to keep the harsh words in his mouth. Everything Mack was saying was true, but it didn't make it any easier to take.

"Look, Cal. You don't have to convince me, I'm the one who recommended you for promotion, remember?"

Cal nodded.

"Okay then, just go home, sit back and wait for this thing to play out." Mack watched his face, but when Cal said nothing more, he continued. "I'm putting Dwight in charge for now, unless you have another recommendation?"

"No, Dwight's your man."

"Good, now that that is settled," he stood and clamped his hands together, "I'm going to get going. And Cal…you know you have to make an appointment with the department shrink."

Cal frowned, but before he could say anything Mack spoke. "Like I told you before, it is all a part of the policy. I don't decide this and neither do you. Just get it over with, so we can put all this behind us."

Cal stood in the same place for several minutes, long after Mack had left. As hard as he'd tried to hold it all together, things had finally spun out of control and he had no one but himself to blame. With the dizziness and hallucinations he'd been experiencing lately, he should've never been on the truck. But his pride wouldn't allow him to stay behind while the whole team went out.

And now, he was not only suspended, his promotion was on the line, and to add insult to injury, he was being forced to see a shrink. That kind of stuff stayed in your file permanently. Now, he had to go home and try to explain all this to Andrea.

Cal sighed with exhaustion, as he began collecting a few of his personal possessions. He'd tried to outrun the tornado, and had gotten flattened by it instead.

Andrea knew something was wrong the minute she turned the corner and saw Cal sitting in the hospital waiting room. He sat with his elbows resting on his knees, and his favorite baseball cap in his hand. As she drew closer, Andrea noticed that he was slapping the hat back and forth between his hands in an unconscious motion, but it was his face that told the tale.

Thinking he was alone, Cal had let his guard down and it was the first time Andrea could ever remember seeing anything like concern on his chocolate-brown face. His soft brown eyes were narrowed in concentration, his front teeth were sunk into his full bottom lip, and his forehead was crinkled with worried lines. Her man was troubled, but if she were to say that to him, she knew he would deny it. Just like Atlas, he carried the weight of the world on his broad shoulders, and insisted on carrying it alone.

Coming closer, she intentionally walked heavier, forcing her small feet to slap, slap against the tiled floor. As expected, the concerned expression disappeared as if it had never been there and Cal stood to greet her with a smile.

"There she is!" He leaned forward and placed a kiss on her cheek. "The sexiest woman in Detroit."

Andrea reached up and wrapped him in her arms. He may not want her to know his pain, but it did not stop her from wanting to comfort him. "Only in Detroit?"

"Did I say Detroit? I meant the world."

"Only the world?"

He leaned back to look in her face. "What? Are you trying to compete with the angels?"

"Okay, I'll take just the world."

He wrapped her even tighter in his arms. "Baby, if I could give it to you I would," he whispered in her ear.

Andrea accepted the tight embrace, reveling in his controlled strength. "What are you doing here?"

He glanced at his watch. "I was in the area, and remembered that you take your lunch break around now. Am I too late?"

"No, perfect timing, actually, but I can't go far. Would you mind eating in the cafeteria?"

"Lead the way."

A few minutes later they sat across the table from one another at one of the small hospital cafeteria tables. Andrea was trying not to laugh as Cal struggled to get comfortable in the small seats.

"Who the hell do they expect to sit in this thing?"

"A normal size man." She chuckled.

He glanced at her sharply, sensing the humor in her eyes was at his expense. He leaned forward to whisper in her ear. "I fit you just fine, don't I?"

Andrea felt the chill run through her whole body at the not-so-subtle reminder of the previous night. "Perfectly." She whispered back, and with a light kiss they each returned to their own sides of the table.

Only then did it occur to her that something about the timing of this luncheon was off. Cal coming to have lunch with her on his off time was a common enough occurrence, but according to her memory, he should be at the firehouse.

"Aren't you on duty?"

"Um, there's been a, um…" Cal didn't realize it would be this hard to say it. "I was suspended."

Andrea tried to squelch the bubble of hope that immediately appeared in her heart. She looked into his eyes, and the anguish she saw there popped the bubble faster than anything else ever could have. "Oh, Cal. I'm so sorry."

"The suspension is just standard procedure," he said with a shrug, trying to minimize the importance of it, but he didn't fool Andrea. As much as she hated it, she knew how important being a firefighter was to him.

"Because of the Hadley building?"

His eyes flashed to hers and he quickly looked away. He had not told her about the fire last week, or the run-in with Jeff. He knew it would just upset her. But there was no way around it now.

"No, because of a fire last week. I um…I froze in the middle of a rescue."

"You froze?" she asked in confusion. Terrifying images of Cal standing like a statue in the mist of an out-of-control blaze raced through her mind.

Cal misunderstood her concern for disdain. "It's not like I *froze* froze," he said defensively. The look in her eyes hurt worse than anything Jeff Collins could've said.

"I just had a delayed reaction time, that's all." He took a bite of his burger, hoping she would not pursue the conversation.

Andrea read his reaction correctly with dismay. Once again, Cal had climbed into that place inside himself, that place she could never go. Anything she asked now would be given a vague, nondescript answer. She chose a safer topic. She reached inside her purse, and pulled out a small stack of invitations.

"Here." She scooted it across the table toward him. "Since you have some free time on your hands."

"What's this?"

"These invitations came back in the mail. I need correct addresses."

Cal frowned as he quickly shuffled through the short stack that contained a couple of childhood friends and a few distant relatives. The last thing he wanted to spend his suspension doing was correct address labels for wedding invitations. He was just not that bored yet.

He pushed the stack back across the table toward Andrea, his nose twisted as if the small pile reeked of some foul odor. "Can't one of your friends do this?"

"How would my friends know your cousin Carolyn's correct street address in Austin, Texas?"

His frown deepened. "You got a point." His eyes flashed over her face as he tried to broach an old argument. "Are you sure you don't want to ask your mother to help—"

"How many times do we have to go over this, Cal? No. I won't ask my mother for help. Involving her means involving my dad."

Several months ago, when Andrea had first

announced her engagement to her parents, it had been a complete disaster.

After they got over the initial shock, they'd immediately begun making plans and preparations for a wedding that her father vowed would be the event of the year. Under different circumstances, Andrea may have been able to see their efforts as generous and kind, except that the plans were being made without any input from her.

Through a fluke, the banquet hall her father had reserved called Andrea by mistake to confirm the date and the reservation for five hundred people. Needless to say, this was a surprise, considering at the time, she and Cal had not even settled on a date, or the amount of people they planned to invite.

In a panic she had taken her anger and outrage straight to Cal, which in hindsight she could see was a mistake. Together they confronted her parents and the situation exploded. That was the one and only time the two men had ever met in the past year, and they'd almost come to blows. Looking back, Andrea understood that what she'd seen as an argument about banquet halls and gowns was really a battle over her, and who would be the most important man in her life going forward. By the end of the evening, Andrea was so distraught she'd not only wanted to break off the engagement, but she also wanted to move as far away from her family as she could get.

It took some time, but like everything else involving her parents, she got over it and began making preparations for the wedding with just the help of a few friends and Marianne, her wedding planner. Now, they were down to less than two months and almost all the arrangements had been made and they were almost ready.

Thinking about the wedding brought to mind something else. Cal had been toying with the idea of telling Andrea about the party the guys had planned. Tommy had tried to talk him out of it, but a part of him was curious to know what she thought.

"Hey, I thought you should know the guys are planning to throw a little bachelor party for me. Would you have a problem with that?"

She smiled and shrugged. "Just so long as you don't forget why you're having the party in the first place. You're off the market, remember?"

"And happy to be." He winked.

Andrea's mind briefly flashed to the last time she'd seen Dina at the firehouse. *By the way, don't*

*worry about that little party they were planning
to throw for Cal. I've taken care of everything.*
Andrea still had no idea what she'd meant.

Cal studied her face across the table while they
continued to eat, noticing the darkened area under
her eyes for the first time and the guilt assailed him.
Of course she wasn't getting any sleep, he thought.
*Between my nightmares, her mother's late-night
calls, and wedding stress, how could she?*

"Hey, I got an idea." Cal smiled as the plan
began formulating in his mind. "Let's take a
weekend trip up to Mackinaw."

Andrea smiled in return. "I would love to, but
we are running out of time. These two months
will fly by."

He reached across the table and took her hands
in his. "When was the last time you had a full
night's sleep?"

"I could ask you the same question."

"Baby, you need a break." He chuckled. "Besides, you'd never forgive me if I let you take
wedding pictures with those little dark spots
under your eyes."

Her eyes widened. "What dark spots?" Within
seconds, she'd whipped out her little compact and
was examining each eye. "Oh no, you're right,

our photos will be horrible. Oh, I can't wait a whole month for Spa Day, I've got to get an emergency appointment." She mumbled to herself the whole while she pulled out her cell phone and phone book and went to work.

Cal just watched with his lips twisting in exasperation, wondering when he would learn to keep his big mouth shut.

"Let's get this party started!" Dwight burst through the door to Tommy's small apartment, carrying a carton of assorted pops and beer. He was feeling quite pleased with the plans he'd made for the evening. It had been a long, uphill battle, but he'd won.

Of course, there would not have been a battle if he hadn't made the critical mistake of leaving the notebook with the party plans lying on the desk of his home office. It had been a momentary slip but had cost him dearly. When Dina had discovered the notes, she'd had a fit. Not a little, wimpy fit, either, no…she had a full-blown, *angry-black-woman-in-full-outrage* kinda fit.

She'd insisted he cancel the party, and in a rare act of fortitude, Dwight refused to give in.

Everyone, including Dwight, knew his wife had him wrapped around her little finger. The guys always teased him about being whipped, which Dwight had no problems with. Although he and Dina had been married for seven years, it was still too easy remember life before her.

Dwight knew he'd been headed down the road to destruction all those years ago. He'd party away the weekend, not much caring what the next day would bring. So, many nights when he'd finally find his way home and fall into bed close to dawn, it was without thought of the next day. Quite frankly, he didn't care if he woke up or not. He just couldn't find the point.

Eight years ago, after a weekend spent in his usual manner, he'd staggered back to his small studio apartment and collapsed, but something strange happened that night. He awoke to find his deceased grandmother sitting on the side of the bed, watching him with loving eyes.

Dwight had rubbed and rubbed his eyes, not believing what he was seeing. He told himself he was just dreaming, but she seemed so real, he could actually feel the soft skin of her hand when she reached down and touched his face.

Dwight had loved his grandmother more than

any human being he'd ever known, and most of his family believed she was the only person he'd ever listened to. In those precious minutes, she talked to him in the same scratchy voice he remembered so well. She made him promise her that he would return to church, and when she disappeared from the room, Dwight fell back on the bed and cried like a baby. Just the way he cried when he'd first lost her.

The next Sunday morning, he cleaned himself up and went back to his childhood church home, which he had not visited in years. He sat down on the only open seat in the back of the church. The young lady sitting next to him scooted over to make room, and he squeezed in. She turned and smiled at him, and Dwight felt something in his stomach do a flip. Eight years later, and her smile could still cause that reaction.

Most of the guys on his engine team never knew *that* Dwight—he'd only joined the team six years ago. But Dina remembered the long, hard road to his salvation, and for what she'd given him, Dwight thought, he could well indulge her.

So, when she'd put her dainty little foot down

and insisted he cancel Cal's party, it had taken everything in him to stand up to her. Cal was his boy—he wasn't about to let him go out without a righteous celebration.

Dina's eyes had widened at the refusal, so unaccustomed to hearing the word *no* come out of his mouth. Then her beautiful brown eyes had narrowed. "We'll see about that!" she stated and then stormed away. Nothing else had been said about it. Of course, he was still sleeping in the guest room when he was off rotation, but it was worth it to send Cal out in style.

Tommy greeted him at the door, and took the tray of drinks. "Is everybody here?" Dwight asked Tommy, hearing Kanye West's "Gold Digger" coming from the other room.

"Everybody but the guest of honor. By the way, it's not a surprise—he knows."

Dwight shrugged with little concern. They had planned out this whole thing where Cavanaugh would pick him up and bring him by Tommy's under some false pretense. But quite frankly, Dwight had been more concerned about the quality of the strippers he'd hired than the surprise element of the party.

A married man for more than seven years, he

was well settled in his chains, but he had to admit this party was as much for him as Cal.

"Food?" Dwight asked.

"Already here. Don't worry, man, you did good. Everything is going smooth as silk."

Dwight moved into the other room, greeting those of their team members who were off duty tonight. He'd tried to schedule the party on a weekend when most of the guys Cal was close to were available.

A short, stockily built man came forward to greet Dwight, and Dwight's eyes lit up at the special surprise he was certain Cal did not know about. "Steve, how was your flight?"

Steve Brown, Cal's little brother, smiled with tired eyes. "Long, but I wouldn't have missed this for the world."

Dwight took the man through the small group, introducing him to everyone he had not already met. Laughing and talking, Dwight suddenly realized that although he saw these guys every day, they very rarely were able to socialize in this manner.

Tommy popped his head in the door. "Cal and Cavanaugh are here," he whispered and darted back out of the room.

Someone turned off the stereo, and the room got very quiet. They heard Tommy talking to someone, then Cavanaugh's voice, followed by Cal's.

Cavanaugh was the first to appear in the doorway. "Forget it, everybody—he knows." There were a few murmured disappointments, and this was what Cal came around the corner to.

Cal laughed. "But thanks for the thought!"

Just then, Steve stepped out from where he'd been standing behind the door. "Bet I'm still a surprise."

Cal spun around, recognizing his brother's voice. "Steve!" He clasped the man in a bear hug. "What the hell you doing here, man?"

"Suffocating," he choked out, before his brother set him back on his feet.

With a big, cheesy grin Cal just took him in head to toe. He hadn't realized how much he missed his only sibling who lived on the other side of the world. Growing up, the two had been inseparable, and his presence was sorely missed in Cal's life.

Soon, the music came back up, and everyone crowded in to offer their congratulations.

Dwight shoved a framed picture of Andrea into his arms laughing, and waving his hands to get everyone's attention. "Now Cal, tonight you may *see* some things…"

Cal just smiled and shook his head at the antics of his friends. A round of hoots followed the statement, everyone was thinking of the entertainment planned for later that evening.

"And Cal," Dwight continued, "you may *feel* some things…"

The group exploded again, and Dwight made a motion to settle them down. "But no matter what you may see and feel tonight, this—" he pointed to the picture "—is to remind you to keep your perspective. Be strong, my bro…"

Cal cocked an eyebrow in silent warning.

And Dwight couldn't finish his statement for the laughter in his voice. After he regained his control, he patted his large friend on the shoulder. "Welcome to the club of the happily married."

"Hear! Hear!" Cavanaugh held his soda can up at the back of the group.

Spontaneously, the group began chanting "Andrea! Andrea! Andrea!"

Cal just waved them away, and went in search of something to drink, the laughter following him out of the room.

Chapter 9

Sometime later, groups had broken off to do pretty much what they did at the firehouse when waiting for a call. Some were playing cards, some playing Tommy's Xbox 360, and many others just sitting around and talking.

Steve was telling Dwight about his excavation in South Africa, and Dwight was struggling to appear interested.

Cal chuckled to himself. His little brother was passionate about his work as an archaeologist, but very few others found it fascinating. He shifted the curtain preparing to step out onto

Tommy's balcony, but he paused when he heard his name. "I don't think Cal's fit for duty any longer." He recognized the voice of Jeff Collins. *What was he doing here?*

"That's a hell of a thing to say about someone you barely know." Cal could hear the anger in Tommy's voice.

"Don't get me wrong. It's just a feeling. I've had it since the day he *lost it* on that staircase, but lately it's like it's intensified a hundred times. I've seen the same thing happen to other firefighters, and afterwards they are never the same. I'm just afraid they are going to put him back on duty and put us all in jeopardy."

"He seemed fine tonight."

"Yeah, well, that's today. What about tomorrow? Are you willing to put your neck on the line with a chief you're unsure of?"

"If that chief is Big Cal, anyday, anytime. And you got a lot of nerve saying this, Jeff, you just got here a few months ago."

"No offense intended," Jeff said in his most soothing tones, and Cal knew he was trying to settle Tommy's ruffled feathers. "It's just an observation, and I'm entitled to my opinion."

Suddenly, the curtain shifted as Jeff prepared

to step through and found himself standing only inches from Cal. His beady eyes widened as much as they could, and his mouth fell open.

Cal just stared at the man. Neither had ever mentioned the incident that occurred in the kitchen of the firehouse. Cal had expected Jeff to report him, but he never did. Without a spoken word, they appeared to have agreed to pretend it didn't happen. This was probably why, Cal assumed, Jeff had been invited. After all, no one was aware that they despised each other.

Because of that, Cal tried very hard to ignore the man. But as soon as he was reinstated, his first plan of action was to get rid of Jeff Collins.

He watched as Jeff's eyes glanced back over his shoulder, and then without another word Jeff went to move around him. Cal was tempted to block his path and confront him, but instead he just stood still as Jeff pushed his way past.

Cal stepped out on the balcony and went to stand next to Tommy who was looking out over the city without showing any indication that he'd overheard the conversation. The noise and music coming from inside the apartment was just a bunch of garbled noises.

Tommy glanced to his side. "What's up?"

"Nice crib," Cal answered.

"It won't be when they get through with it." He nodded over his shoulder.

"So, when are the strippers supposed to get here?" Cal tried to make small talk to keep from asking the questions he really wanted to ask.

"Any minute now, according to Dwight."

Just then, someone called through the curtain. "Hey, Tommy, someone's at the door, I think it's the girls."

"Be right there." Tommy turned to leave, then paused. "Hey Cal…"

"Yeah?"

"Watch your back with Jeff."

Cal stiffened, wondering if more was said than what he'd overheard. "Why do you say that?"

Tommy started to say something then stopped. "Just trust me when I say he's up to no good." He turned and headed back into the apartment.

Cal stood alone on the balcony for a while, contemplating everything that had happened in the past few weeks. Some part of him had not wanted to come here tonight, unsure of how his coworkers would see him after the last fire and his suspension. But everyone had greeted him with slaps on the back and genuine admiration in their eyes.

When he reentered the apartment, the guys were clearing away the card tables, and opening up the middle of the floor. There was an excitement and anticipation in the air that Cal just couldn't manage to work up himself. He could give a few smiles and laughs, but genuine pleasure was something that was eluding him lately.

"Is it the girls?" someone asked excitedly, seeing Tommy reenter the room alone and with a slightly befuddled expression on his face.

"Um, yeah," Tommy answered evasively, working his way around the room to Dwight. "Dwight, can I talk to you for a moment?"

Cal came up behind the two men with their heads huddled together.

"Where exactly did you find these dancers?" Tommy was asking Dwight.

"The phone book under exotic dancers. Why?"

Tommy twisted his mouth. "I don't know, but something about them just doesn't seem... *exotic enough*."

Dwight frowned in disappointment. "Damn. They're ugly, aren't they?"

"No, no," Tommy answered quickly. "They are all quite lovely, it's just...well, for one, they are all dressed in different colored tights."

"Tights?" Cal and Dwight's baritone voices together brought almost every head in the room around.

"Tights?" Dwight whispered, still not quite understanding. "What is that? A fancy name for a G-string?"

"I didn't see anything resembling a G-string."

The crowd behind them was beginning to grumble impatiently. "Bring on the booty shakers!" someone called from across the room. Soon the chant was taken up and the whole room was vibrating with energy and anticipation.

Dwight sighed. "Well, whatever they are dressed in we better let them come on out before we have a riot up in here."

"Your call," Tommy said with a shrug and headed back to inform the girls.

Dwight put up his hands. "All right, everyone, settle down. The show is about to begin. But understand me, fellows." His voice dropped all humor. "These young women *will be* treated with respect. Am I making myself clear?" The statement was followed by murmured agreement.

Cal touched him on the shoulder. "Dwight, can I say something?"

Dwight stepped aside to give him the floor. "I

would just like to say I really appreciate all of this." He gestured to the room at large. "And all you guys for doing this for me. I know things have been a little strained lately, but I just wanted you all to know how much I appreciate all your support!" He let his eyes flash across Jeff's face, and the man quickly looked away.

Suddenly, there was a loud boom coming from the stereo, as the dancers' music began. The boom was followed by a soft string instrumental. The guys settled down and waited for the show to begin.

Finally, a flowing, colorful line of five women entered, dressed head to toe in colored leotards, the tight bun hairstyle identical on each head. They danced across the floor like a line of balle-rinas entering the stage, each carried a scarf that they used for different positioning.

They stopped suddenly, and took up different positions, one lifting her leg around her neck, another doing a full body split, two others forming the letter *K* and the fifth stepping off to the side and reciting poetry.

Within five minutes of the performance, they'd managed to leave their audience speechless.

KIMANI PRESS™

An Important Message from the Publisher

Dear Reader,

Because you've chosen to read one of our fine novels, I'd like to say "thank you"! And, as a special way to say thank you, I'm offering to send you two Kimani Romance™ novels and two surprise gifts – absolutely FREE! These books will keep it real with true-to-life African-American characters that turn up the heat and sizzle with passion.

Please enjoy the free books and gifts with our compliments...

Linda Gill

Publisher, Kimani Press

Peel off Seal and Place Inside...

PUBLISHERS FREE GIFTS SEAL THANK YOU

We'd like to send you two free books to introduce you to our new line – Kimani Romance™! These novels feature strong, sexy women and African-American heroes that are charming, loving and true. Our authors fill each page with exceptional dialogue, exciting plot twists, and enough sizzling romance to keep you riveted until the very end!

KIMANI ROMANCE ... LOVE'S ULTIMATE DESTINATION

Your two books have a combined cover price o $11.98 in the U.S. and $13.98 in Canada, but are yours **FREE!** We' even send you two wonderful surprise gifts. You can't lose

THE EDITOR'S "THANK YOU" FREE GIFTS INCLUDE:

▶ Two NEW Kimani Romance™ Novels

▶ Two exciting surprise gifts

YES! I have placed my Editor's "Thank You" Free Gifts seal in the space provided at right. Please send me 2 FREE books, and my 2 FREE Mystery Gifts. I understand that I am under no obligation to purchase anything further, as explained on the back of this card.

PLACE
FREE GIFTS
SEAL
HERE

168 XDL ELWZ   368 XDL ELXZ

FIRST NAME

LAST NAME

ADDRESS

APT.#

CITY

STATE/PROV.

ZIP/POSTAL CODE

Thank You!

The Reader Service — Here's How It Works:

Accepting your 2 free books and 2 free gifts places you under no obligation to buy anything. You may keep the books and gifts and return the shipping statement marked "cancel." If you do not cancel, about a month later we'll send you 4 additional books and bill you just $4.69 each in the U.S. or $5.24 each in Canada, plus 25¢ shipping & handling per book and applicable taxes if any." That's the complete price and — compared to cover prices of $5.99 each in the U.S. and $6.99 each in Canada — it's quite a bargain! You may cancel at any time; but if you choose to continue, every month we'll send you 4 more books, which you may either purchase at the discount price or return to us and cancel your subscription.

*Terms and prices subject to change without notice. Sales tax applicable in N.Y. Canadian residents will be charged applicable provincial taxes and GST. All orders subject to approval. Books received may vary. Credit or debit balances in a customer's account(s) may be offset by any other outstanding balance owed by or to the customer. Please allow 4 to 6 weeks for delivery.

If offer card is missing write to: The Reader Service, 3010 Walden Ave., P.O. Box 1867, Buffalo, NY 14240-1867

BUSINESS REPLY MAIL
FIRST-CLASS MAIL   PERMIT NO. 717-003   BUFFALO, NY

POSTAGE WILL BE PAID BY ADDRESSEE

THE READER SERVICE
3010 WALDEN AVE
PO BOX 1867
BUFFALO NY 14240-9952

NO POSTAGE
NECESSARY
IF MAILED
IN THE
UNITED STATES

"What the hell is this?" someone whined into the silence, and because of the silence the statement seemed even harsher.

The girls stopped and turned startled eyes on their host, and Dwight stepped forward scratching his chin. Probably the only one in the room with any idea of what was going on, and even he was not sure. He needed to have it confirmed.

"Ladies, are you by any chance from a company called Midnight Rendezvous?"

The poet spoke for the group. "No, we're from Words in Motion, an interpretive dance company."

Dwight nodded as his first suspicion was confirmed. "And who hired you?"

They each looked one to the other. "Um, our agent set it up."

"I see, I see." He clapped his hands together in one hard slap, already contemplating the various ways of getting back at his wife. "Thank you ladies, you can go now."

With one final glance at the dumbfounded group, the poet, who seemed to be the leader, took their CD from the stereo and started out of the room. The others followed quietly.

"Okay, what just happened?" someone blurted out.

"I don't know, but those were definitely not booty shakers."

"Come on Dwight, you promised us a show."

In the midst of what was quickly becoming a mob mentality, a burst of deep, rumbling laughter stopped everyone. They all turned to see Cal curled on his side, laughing so hard he seemed to be having trouble breathing.

Dwight came to stand over his trembling form. "Have you lost your mind?"

Cal looked up at Dwight. "You promised me a bachelor party I would not soon forget, and man, did you deliver on the promise."

Unable to resist his good humor, Dwight shook his head and smiled. "I am a man of my word."

Finally, getting the laughter under control, Cal sat up. "Thanks, man, you don't know how much I needed this."

Realizing there would be no exotic dancers, the groups went back to their previous activities, playing cards until they found a good game on TV. The party didn't break up until well into the morning and everyone left satisfied that they'd given Cal an *almost* perfect send-off.

Chapter 10

Cal picked his way through the debris, his thoughts centered on the fire damage that surrounded him on every side. Something wasn't right about the scene. This had been the fourth fire in the same number of days. That in itself was not so unusual, given the above-average temperatures they'd been experiencing that summer. But combine that with the similarities in each case, and the situation reeked of foul play.

Just then, he noticed the fire marshal entering the opening that was once a doorway. "Noel!" he called to the familiar man.

Noel nodded in greeting before stepping over a crushed pile of what were once cereal boxes. "What's up, man? I heard you were…out for a while."

Cal stiffened, realizing that word of his suspension was apparently making its way through the department and into other firehouses.

"Yeah, just until they complete their probe." He waved it off, hoping he sounded more unconcerned than he felt. "What's your take on this?" Cal gestured to the destruction surrounding them.

"Don't know. Just got here."

"Did you work the fire at that nail shop on Gratiot yesterday afternoon?"

Noel shook his head in denial, his eyes surveying the work ahead of him. He was breaking down the scene and the way he intended to divide his manpower, even as he carried on the conversation with his friend.

"Well, let's just say the aftermath looked a lot like this place," Cal continued. "And the liquor store on Vandyke the day before, and the doctor's office on east Jefferson the day before that."

By now he had the fire marshal's complete attention. "You thinking arson?"

"It was always after hours when the places

were closed and no one could get hurt, and it was always commercial buildings, not private homes."

Noel gave Cal an unreadable look. "How do you know all this?"

"I visited the scenes and read the reports, as well."

Noel just continued to stare.

"Look, Noel, the fire that got me suspended looked a lot like this. It's what first made me suspicious. If there is an arsonist in my district, I want to know. This guy may've cost me my badge."

Okay, it was making sense now, Noel thought. If he were in Cal's shoes he would probably be doing the same thing. Tilting his head to the side, he mentally reviewed what he knew about those other fires. Many times, his subordinates went out to inspect without him, and he thought that was probably the case with the nail shop and the doctor's office, since he had no memory of reviewing the reports. But he did remember the liquor store. He was still in the process of determining the cause. He'd already ruled out accidental. What Cal was saying only confirmed his own suspicions, and now he knew there were probably other deliberately set fires, as well.

"I already suspected something was up with that liquor store fire, but thanks for the heads-up. I'll definitely take that into consideration during my investigation." He frowned, just remembering something. "Did you say the nail shop was on Gratiot?"

Cal nodded.

"And the doctor's office on East Jefferson?"

Cal nodded again.

"That explains it. Those are both outside my jurisdiction. But I'll contact the marshal for that district and get copies of the reports." He shook his head sadly. "The last thing I need is an arsonist in the area. Hell, we get enough work with legitimate cases."

Cal chuckled. "I heard that. Can you let me know what you find out?"

When he received no answer, he realized Noel's attentions were distracted by Marty, who was knocking down the fragile outer wall of the building some distance away.

"How's St. John treating her?" Noel asked the question, knowing Cal would understand his interest.

"Good, as far as I know. She seems happy."

Noel looked away quickly. "Good." He forced

a weak smile. "I'm happy for her. And thanks again for the info." He turned and began moving across the room to begin his inspection. "I'll give you a call," he called over his shoulder at the last minute.

Cal watched the other man walk away with slumped shoulders that reminded him he wasn't the only one with problems.

"Cal, have you ever heard of post-traumatic stress disorder?"

Cal frowned at Chet Butler, one of the many department shrinks. Of course he'd heard of PTSD, what firefighter or cop had not? "Yeah, but what has that got to do with me?"

Chet, a small, quiet man, cleared his throat loudly, already knowing what Cal's reaction was going to be. But he pushed ahead anyway. "That is my diagnosis. I believe you are suffering from PTSD."

"What? Are you kidding me?" Cal shot to his feet to tower over the man. "After only three sessions you come up with this?"

Chet looked up at the giant standing over him. "Cal, sit down, please."

Cal balled his fist at his side trying to regain

control of his temper. He flopped back down in the chair and sighed. "You're wrong Doc." He buried his head in his hands.

Chet just waited for the other man to accept what was blatantly obvious. The diagnosis of PTSD was always the most resisted by firefighters, who often reacted as if he'd just accused them of having a mental breakdown. Because of the symptoms, PTSD had a reputation of being a career ender, and it was always met with outrage, disbelief and sometimes violence. And yet, it was the most common diagnosis throughout the fire department.

For men and women who dragged charred bodies out of burning buildings on a daily basis, it was only natural that eventually the stress of what they did would take its toll. And the condition could easily be treated with therapy and sometimes medication. Chet was quite proud of the fact that most of his patients were able to return to active duty in a relatively short amount of time. There was always the initial shock of the diagnosis and the refusal to accept it. But once they got beyond that, he was able to help them.

Right now, Cal was just at the acceptance stage. Chet knew it would take time. "Cal, all the symptoms point to PTSD—the dizziness, the hallucinations, the nightmares."

Cal's brown eyes came up to meet his, and Chet could see the torment behind them. "That can't be." Cal shook his head adamantly. "No, you're wrong."

"Cal, I know what you are thinking, but PTSD is not what you think it is. No one is saying you are crazy, or have to give up your career. It is entirely treatable."

Cal shot to his feet again. "You're wrong." The words were said with no anger, but with absolute conviction. He turned and headed toward the door.

"Cal!" Chet called realizing his patient was leaving. He stood. "Where are you going? We still have fifteen minutes left in our session."

"Home, I need to…" Cal found his mind was too muddled to form coherent thought. "I need to get out of here."

"Cal, I'm gonna have to give Mack my diagnosis soon. Can't we just talk a little more, maybe come to some sort of understanding regarding what is neces—Cal! Please come ba—"

Chet watched the door swing shut behind the man and shook his head. This was always the hardest part of the job. Firefighters and cops used confidence and self-assuredness like a shield and sword. What the average citizen saw as cocky arrogance, he understood was a necessity to get the job done. Insecure, self-doubting people did not run into burning buildings or face armed criminals. No, these men and women *needed* to believe in their own indestructibility.

Before he'd actually met the man, Chet had heard of Big Cal Brown through rumors of his heroics. He knew that for someone like Cal his diagnosis would be especially hard to accept. He could only hope the man would eventually accept the inevitable. In order to become the fireman he once was, he would have to accept professional help.

Chapter 11

Andrea looked at her watch again before zipping up her overnight tote and setting it on the floor near the door. She hadn't heard from Cal all morning, and his appointment with the department psychiatrist had ended three hours ago. She headed back into the bedroom and picked up the phone on her bedside table. She dialed his cell phone once more, but still there was no answer.

It was getting late, and she was getting worried. They were supposed to be on the road headed north to Mackinaw Island for the weekend two hours ago, and she was certain Cal re-

membered the time they agreed on. She picked
up the phone to call the firehouse, thinking
maybe he'd stopped by there to see the guys on
his way back and lost track of the time. She'd
dialed the first four digits when she heard a key
in the front door lock.

She hurried back into the living room, where
she saw Cal had already picked up two of the
three bags sitting by the front entrance, and was
heading back out the door with them.

She grabbed her purse off the dinette table
and followed him out. "Where were you?"

He glanced back over his shoulder at her as he
circled the vehicle. "Where I was supposed to be,
down at mental, seeing the shrink."

Andrea stopped dead in her tracks hearing the
gruff tone of his voice. This wasn't the *Hey, baby,
let's get on the road and have some fun* voice.
No, this was the *Leave me the hell alone* voice.

In the beginning of their relationship, that
voice had stopped her in her tracks more than
once. Growing up with Andrew Chenault, she
had good reason to be wary. But now, she knew
no matter how intimidating Cal may be in voice
and form, he would never hurt her.

"So…what happened?" She tossed her handbag

on the front passenger seat through the partially opened window and walked around to the back of the truck where Cal was lowering the rear gate.

"He obviously doesn't know what he's talking about," he announced casually, as he began loading their suitcases onto the bed of the truck. "He said I have PTSD."

Andrea felt something like a chill on the wind behind the acronym. After a year of listening to firehouse conversations, she knew PTSD was like a death sentence to a firefighter. "What did you say?"

"Just what I told you, he obviously doesn't know what he's talking about."

"Cal, he had to be using some kind of insight. The man has had years of professional training. I'm sure he wouldn't just make a declaration like that unless he had something to base it on. I know you're not the only firefighter he's ever diagnosed with this."

Cal slammed the gate shut and spun around. "You sure as hell are eager to agree with him! Why don't you go down there and help him write the report. I'm sure he could use your *input* regarding the nightmares." With that sarcastic statement, Cal stormed back into the house.

Andrea waited for her heart to stop pounding.

She had to tread lightly here. He was hurting and one wrong word would cause him to set in his heels against the idea that he may have post traumatic stress disorder.

When she entered the living room, Cal was sitting on the couch. His long legs were stretched out in front of him and crossed at the ankles. The remote control dangled carelessly from his fingers, as his thumb occasionally grazed over the buttons.

"Mackinaw Island is a three-hour ride," she said quietly. "Don't you think we should get started?"

"I'm starting to think this whole weekend getaway is a bad idea. I mean, if you are just going to hound me the whole time, hell, we can stay home and do that."

That did it. Wounded bear or no wounded bear, she'd had enough of his snide remarks. She stood in the doorway in silence for several minutes, watching him channel surf before finally crossing the room to the television and turning it off.

"I understand you are angry and frustrated and have a lot on your mind, but you *will not* take it out on me."

When she turned to face him, Cal saw a look in her eyes that he'd never seen before. It was a combination of hurt and anger, disappointment and pain.

"Cal, face it…whatever is going on with you, you can't handle it alone, and as much as I want to, *I don't know how* to help you. You need this man's help, this *doctor's* help in understanding what is going on in your mind."

He stood and stretched out his long arms. "Look at me, Andrea. Do you think anyone has ever offered to help me with anything in my life? People take one look at me and decide that I am the *least* helpless person they've ever met. I've always had to do it on my own, even when I needed help. So I've learned to survive whatever life threw my way and I'll survive this, whatever this is."

They stood on opposite sides of the room for several seconds, staring at one another in a silent showdown.

Finally, Cal spoke. "I'm sorry I snapped at you. I just ask that you let me handle this my way. Can you do that?"

"I don't know." She shook her head sadly. "Your way seems to be killing us."

Cal sighed heavily. "Andrea, I don't know how much longer I will be allowed to stay with the department. If this shrink gives me a negative eval,

I'm done. Which means I am not only out of a job, but a job I love." He slumped down on the couch again and huffed. "Who am I kidding? All my life I dreamed of being a firefighter. And once I was accepted by the academy, I never looked back. This is more than a job, Andrea. This is who I am, and honestly, I don't know who I will be once it is gone."

"You'll be Calvin Brown, the man I love. Turnout gear does not define you!" Andrea crossed the room and stood in front of him. "You're not your job or your reputation. Regardless of what you are doing for a living, you will still be the man you are today. I know you love being a firefighter, but baby…if you can't do it, then life goes on."

"Maybe for you, and maybe even for the rest of the world, but for me…I don't know what else I would do."

She looked up into his eyes, needing to express everything she felt in her heart. "Then we will find out together."

A week later, Cal was back at the firehouse and this time he was on a mission. Tucked beneath his arm was a notebook containing notes he'd taken earlier that morning when he'd spoken with Noel.

Apparently, they did indeed have a firebug in their midst, and accordingly to Noel it was someone who had access to the type of accelerant used by the department. When he heard that, Cal suddenly remembered the day he saw Jeff coming up the stairs with the can of accelerant cradled in his arm.

When Cal reached the top of the stairs, Tommy was coming toward him. "Hey, man, when are we doing tuxedo fittings?"

"Wednesday evening," Cal gave a distracted answer as his eyes surveyed the area. "You know where Jeff is?"

Something about his face must've given away his inner rage, because Tommy's eyes widened in surprise.

"Yeah, but given that look on your face, I don't know if I should tell you."

Cal forced a laugh. "It's okay, man, just got a lot on my mind."

Tommy's eyes narrowed in suspicion, and Cal knew he wasn't buying it. His friend knew him too well. "Hmph, he's in the kitchen."

"Thanks, man." Cal patted the other man on the

shoulder as he moved past him toward the kitchen. As soon as he entered he found Jeff standing at the stove, concentrating on the grilled cheese sandwich that was slow cooking in a skillet.

His head came up at Cal's entry and his eyes instantly hardened. "What are you doing here? Only firefighters allowed."

"Just visited some friends, seeing how things have been going in my absence." Cal studied the man's tight back as he leaned against the sink. "Dwight was telling me you have really become a team player since I've been gone."

Jeff glanced over his shoulder with narrowed eyes. "Is that right?" His voice was laced with suspicion.

Cal's mouth twisted. "Yeah. So, what's new?"

Jeff glanced at him again, his eyebrows crinkled in confusion and Cal knew he was trying to make sense of the sudden truce.

"Nothing new, and yourself?"

"Nothing much. Been catching up on my reading."

"Really?" Jeff asked with little interest, while flipping his sandwich in the skillet.

"Yeah, I'm reading this really interesting book right now about a firefighter who is secretly an arsonist." Cal watched in satisfaction as Jeff's hand stopped in midair above the skillet.

"Oh?"

"Yeah, it seems he had some personal beef with his chief." Cal's eyes narrowed on the other man's back. "Haven't figured out what it is yet. But anyway, this firefighter slash arsonist decided to take out his anger by staging fires in his district."

Jeff turned to fully face him for the first time since he'd entered the kitchen. "Why would he do that?"

Cal tilted his head thoughtfully, but never took his eyes off Jeff's face. "Don't know, haven't gotten that far in the book...yet."

Something in Jeff's eyes shifted, and Cal knew the man was finally beginning to understand that he wouldn't be here if he didn't have something.

"So?" Jeff asked, reaching back to turn off the skillet.

"So, what?"

"So, how do they catch the guy?"

The man was worried. It was written all over his face. Cal turned from the sink and smiled wickedly. "I don't want to give that away. I mean, what if you decide to borrow the book one day?"

Jeff's eyes narrowed. "If you got something to say, Cal, just say it."

Cal shrugged, feeling like a bored cat who'd found a mouse to play with. Being suspended was incredibly hard to deal with, but it felt good to have a purpose again. One way or the other, he would prove that Jeff was the arsonist, but knowing which accelerant was used, and happening to see Jeff with a can one time was simply not enough. No, as much as he wanted to take the guy down, he would have to bide his time.

"Nothing to say." He smiled evilly. "Just telling you about a book I'm reading. Kinda anxious to get to the end though, you know...the part where they catch the guy." He turned and walked out of the kitchen.

Chapter 12

Cal sat on the back terrace of the elegant mini mansion in the plush suburb neighborhood waiting patiently while the man across from him read his notes. He surveyed the decorative shrubs that surrounded the large in-ground pool some twenty feet from where they sat. He'd been to the house a hundred times in the past year and still marveled that some people lived this way. Especially when the people were as real and down-to-earth as Marty and Cavanaugh.

Of course, Cavanaugh, having been born and bred into this sort of lifestyle, thought nothing of it. Cal still chuckled, remembering how Cavanaugh had described their new home as a nice, family-style home. Maybe if you were raising the Jackson Five, Cal thought.

Finally, Cavanaugh finished reading and pushed the notebook back across the table to his friend. "And you think this Jeff guy is the arsonist?" His dark eyes widened in surprise.

"We've had an outbreak of fires in our district since he arrived, all of them suspicious. Even Noel thinks we have an arsonist in the area."

"Cal, do you know what you are saying?" Cavanaugh stood and crossed to the open bar. He continued to speak with his back to Cal. "A firefighter turned arsonist…you better be sure you know what you are talking about before you make an accusation like that." He lifted a small teapot from the warmer and offered it to Cal.

Cal shook his head, rejecting the offer of tea. "I don't have any proof, that's the only reason I haven't said anything. That's why I'm here. I need your help."

"What kind of help?"

"I can't trust anyone at the firehouse. They all think I'm losing it. I need outside help."

Cal noticed Cavanaugh's expression had darkened, and knowing exactly what caused that look, he put up a hand in defense. "I know Marty would never betray me, but she might say something to the wrong person by mistake."

"Not if you tell her not to."

"Please, Cavanaugh, I would just feel better if no one at the firehouse knew."

"Knew what?"

"Before I say anything more, I need some assurance. Are you agreeing to help me?"

"I'm not agreeing to anything until I know what you expect of me. I mean, you are asking me to keep secrets from my wife. You have to have a damn good reason to ask something like that of me."

"How about my life? Is that a good enough reason?"

Cavanaugh came back and sat across from the other man. "You think this man is trying to kill you?"

"I think...that may be a possibility. There's something about the way that guy looks at me." He shook his head, unable to find the right words. "There is some serious hate in it."

"But why? He just met you a few months ago."

"I've been asking myself that same question

since I first noticed it. Maybe I met him some-
where before. Maybe I just don't remember him.
I don't know, but whatever it is, if I'm not careful,
I may not be around to find out."

Cavanaugh sat quietly contemplating this
stunning news. "What do you need from me?"

"Help me find out who this guy really is. All
I know is what I have in his personnel file. That
just outlines his career. I want to know about
him. If I crossed this guy, I don't think it was on
the job."

"That shouldn't be so difficult. I'll ask JJ—
you remember the detective Marty had following
me?"

"Oh yeah, I had forgotten about him. Thanks
man, I appreciate your help."

"Don't thank me too quickly. I understand
how you feel about keeping this quiet, especially
considering your suspension and everything. But
I'm not hearing anything so far that persuades me
to keep this from Marty. She would never betray
you. In fact, it may be good to have at least one
person in the firehouse you can trust."

Cal twisted his mouth, wondering how much
this decision would hinder his plans. "So, what
are you saying? You are going to **tell Marty**?"

"No. But if she asks I won't lie to her."

Cal nodded. "That's fair." He stood to leave. "I really appreciate your help, man."

As Cavanaugh walked his friend to the door, he wondered over everything he'd been told. He was making plans to call JJ as soon as Cal left. If this Jeff Collins was an arsonist, they needed to know that right away. If he was a threat to Cal, they needed to know that even sooner.

The two men shook hands in the doorway. "Cal," Cavanaugh called to his friend before he reached his truck parked in the horseshoe driveway. "Just…just watch your back, man."

Cal smiled and lifted an eyebrow in agreement. "I plan to."

"Cal…Cal." Cal could hear the voice calling, but initially resisted. Following the voice meant he would have to leave this place of peace, this place of rest.

"Cal."

His eyes fluttered involuntarily as he struggled out of the deep slumber.

"Cal." He opened his eyes, and finally focused on Andrea standing over him. He looked in every direction, trying to get his bearings. He was on the couch in his office at the firehouse. He struggled into a sitting position.

"What am I doing here?" he asked, looking around in confusion.

"That's what I would like to know."

He looked down at the files strewn across the leather couch. "Must've fallen asleep while I was looking through these files." He rubbed his eyes, still trying to pull himself out of what felt like a drugged state. He could see a shadow standing behind Andrea, and finally focused on Marty's concerned face.

Andrea followed his eyes. "She told me you were here. Thanks, Marty. Can you leave us alone for a minute?"

With a nod, Marty let herself out of the room and pulled the door closed behind her.

"Cal, what are you doing? If Mack or some other high ranking officer found you here going through these files, they could bring criminal charges—"

"You don't have to read me the code, Andrea."

"Then what is this all about, Cal?" She held up a handful of files. "Is this more important than us? Because that is what you are jeopardizing, our future!"

He stood and tried to balance himself. Cal had decided not to say anything to Andrea regarding his suspicions until he heard from Cavanaugh. With the suspension and upcoming wedding, and her constant concern for her mother's safety, he felt she had enough to worry about. But now, that path left him with no way to explain his strange behavior.

"Andrea, let's just talk about this at home."

"No, Cal, I've had enough. It's like you're obsessed with being a fireman!"

He sighed. "This isn't about being a fireman."

"Then what is it about? Because I do not understand."

He stood in stony silence. No, she *didn't* understand. How could she? She wasn't the one waking in the middle of the night in a cold sweat. She wasn't the one seeing things that were not there. She wasn't the one losing her mind.

"What do you want me to say, Andrea?" Cal felt his heart twisting inside his chest as the water began to form in her eyes.

"Say…say that you love me more than this firehouse. Say that being my husband is more important than being a fireman."

Cal gasped at the look of hurt and pain in her

eyes. *Where is this coming from?* Up until that moment Cal had not considered how the situation must look to her. After everything they'd gone through in the past few months, the nightmares, the suspension, and now she was finding him sleeping at the firehouse. It was only reasonable she would have doubts about what was important to him.

"Baby, what are you talking about? Of course I love you more than the job."

"Yeah, sure Cal…whatever." Andrea shook her head in defeat, turned toward the door, and Cal was suddenly in front of her. He reached out and pulled her hard again his chest. Tilting her head, his mouth sought hers. Gently at first, then with more pressure as he felt her begin to relax in his arms.

He ran his warm tongue across her bottom lip coaxing her to open and she did. Her lips parted and her arms came up around his neck. There was a sudden surge of power coursing through Cal's body. He felt her hesitation and knew she was still angry and did not want to respond, but could no more resist him than he could resist her.

She took a deep breath and pushed against his chest to free herself from his arms. "No, it won't be that easy this time. You can't kiss your way out of this, Cal." She backed away, and he followed until she found herself pinned against the door.

Cal only stopped when his muscular chest was pressed against her soft breasts, and even then he continued to push gently against her. Wanting her to understand what he could not tell her with words. That there was nothing in the world more important to him that her.

"I love you, Andrea, and that comes before anything else." He kissed her again, fighting not to overwhelm her with his intense emotions. His lips trailed down the smooth, sweet-smelling skin of her neck. And he paused there, only long enough to run his tongue over a fast thumping vein. Then continued his exploration as his kisses found their way along her collarbone and toward the peek of cleavage just above her thin, low-necked sweater.

"Oh, Cal. What are we going to do?" There was so much anguish in her voice as her small arms came up and wrapped around his head.

"We're going to love each other, and let everything else take care of itself." His large finger worked the button fly of her jeans with deft precision. He quickly slipped his hands inside the coarse material and her soft, rounded hips.

Unable to stop the building passion, Andrea kissed him on every part of his body, the top of his head, his shoulders, and his arms, anywhere she could reach while wiggling out of the jeans and panties Cal was sliding down her legs.

"No matter what happens, never doubt that I love you," he whispered against her ear, right before he took her firm thighs in his hands and lifted them around his waist.

His hot mouth latched on to her neck, and all Andrea heard was the sharp unzipping sound, followed by the crinkling of paper, and then he was there, pushing against her wet opening.

Andrea lifted her body wanting to help guide him inside of her. She braced herself on his shoulders and bit her bottom lip to stifle a glorious groan as he entered her. She felt his hands squeezing her bottom as he tightened his hold. With one powerful thrust he lowered her down on his penis, burying himself as deep inside as possible.

Remembering where they were, Andrea sunk her teeth into his shoulder to keep from crying out. This was not the answer to their troubles, intellectually she knew that, but the intense sensation coursing through her entire being as the man she loved stroked her inside had nothing to do with intellect. It was pure animal passion.

Andrea could feel the pressure building, the pinnacle of pleasure within reach. Her breathing became shorter as her pounding heart sped even more. It was almost there…almost. Her mouth fell open as she struggled to breathe, she felt as if she were drowning…

"Hold on, baby," Cal whispered against her ear, and his hands squeezed her flesh even harder. She gripped his shoulders as he pounded into her body, again and again. Suddenly, she exploded. Her back arched, and a cry of pleasure escaped her mouth. Cal buried his head against her neck, pushed himself deep inside her body once, twice, and then he followed her over the edge.

Chapter 13

"All right, everyone, positions!" Marianne Kenton, one of Detroit's most noted wedding planners, clapped her hands loudly. "Positions, everyone!"

The group mingling around the church moved into place as they'd been instructed earlier. All participants in the procession moved outside the large double doors. They paired up in the order most of them had come to memorize.

Three sets of couples, the maid of honor and the best man, followed by two bridesmaids and groomsmen. All dressed in colors similar to those that decorated the small church. Marianne watched the group form with hawklike intensity and satisfaction.

The bride, in her misguided ignorance, had wanted to use the traditional colors of burgundy and white, but it hadn't been hard to bulldoze her into something more unusual. Marianne had wanted iridescent tangerine and deep purple. The pair finally came together on pastel apricot and white.

Of course, most people did not typically have pastel apricot in their wardrobes so the overall effect of the rehearsal was not exactly what she wanted. She also did not like the fact that due to the work schedule of some of the wedding party members they were forced to schedule the rehearsal a week before the wedding. But after fifteen years in the business, Marianne learned to roll with the punches. She'd planned over four hundred weddings in her career with care and precision. Each and every one had been a personal experience. This one was no exception. She silently reminded herself that this was only a rehearsal. The actual ceremony would be perfect.

Pushing her large glasses back up on her nose, the planner looked in every direction, making mental notes of the final touches that needed to be added. The pews were sectioned off with white streamers. Beautiful gladiolas in white and bright orange lined the altar. She took in the other minor details before returning her attention to the group congregating outside the entrance. They were getting restless, and her neat formation was falling apart.

"All right, everyone. We are about to start the march. Remember, Marty and Cavanaugh, once the music starts count to twenty-five before you begin." She clapped loudly to get everyone's attention once again, glancing back at the organ, she gasped in alarm. "Where's my pianist?"

"Here I am!" called the short, rotund woman rushing back into the sanctuary, while busily tucking her blouse back into her skirt. "Sorry," she smiled shyly, taking her seat at the bench.

Marianne's eyes narrowed behind her glasses. "Make sure on Sunday you take care of all the essentials *before* the ceremony begins."

Eyebrows rose, and most took a mental note to remember to empty their bladders before the ceremony on Sunday rather than risk incurring Marianne's wrath.

Marianne gestured to the pianist to begin the

wedding march. "All right, Cavanaugh and Marty." She motioned for the maid of honor and best man to begin moving forward.

The lovely couple leading the procession stepped through the doors and into the church. Both tall and slender, with eyes only for one another, they looked as if they'd walked right off the pages of a fashion magazine. They began down the aisle, moving in rhythm with the music. "Remember, Tommy and Jill, count to twenty-five before stepping in behind them."

The couple, who were visibly uncomfortable with each other, held their place for several seconds. Suddenly, Jill stepped forward while Tommy remained standing in place.

Tommy yanked hard, using his greater strength to pull his anxious partner back to his side. "*She said* twenty-five," he hissed.

"I did count to twenty-five," Jill hissed back, and yanked hard on his arm to set him in motion.

Tommy instinctively pulled back only for a moment, before realizing they were holding up the procession and allowed himself to be pulled forward.

The planner simply shook her head, the couple had been arguing all evening. She could only hope they did not ruin her beautiful wedding. "All right, Dina and Dwight." She motioned for the third couple.

The third couple stepped through the doors in synchronized steps. Having stood up many times before, they were veterans to the process. After ten years of marriage, their harmonious union needed no synchronization.

Marilyn smiled in approval. This would work, she thought. *Despite* Jill and Tommy, as long as Dina and Dwight brought up the rear, it would work. She watched with pride as the small procession marched steadily down the aisle. Her perfect record of success was in no danger.

At the end of the altar stood Cal, waiting and watching for the woman he loved to appear in the doorway. His heart was in his throat, his palms were clammy, and standing with both feet planted firmly on the ground Cal had the sudden feeling of falling. He felt lightheaded and dizzy and was certain he was about to fall out. Only his determination and pride kept him standing upright.

He felt the bracing hand of his brother Steve touch his sleeve. "You okay?"

Cal nodded brusquely, not wanting to draw any attention to his weakness.

Steve studied his profile silently for several seconds before turning his attention back to the procession.

"All right, Andrea," Marianne called to the bride, standing just outside view of the double doors.

Andrea stepped through the doorway dressed in a soft, apricot orange dress with a V-neck and tie belt. Her midlength jet-black hair was twisted up in a French roll, and her makeup was minimal, as always. She quickly scanned the front of the church until she found Cal.

Their eyes locked across the empty church. The stress of the past few weeks was written on each face, and they each saw it in the other.

Andrea was staring at the man she knew would always hold her heart, and remembering the wonder and magic of when they'd first met. The world was filled with hope and possibility then…and now, here she was only a week before her wedding, what was supposed to be the happiest time of her life, and she was more confused and unhappy than she had been in months.

The only thing she did know with absolute clarity was that she loved the man. With every drop of blood in her body, she absolutely adored him. But was it enough? Would happy memories be enough to comfort a devastated widow? Would the stirrings of past desire conquer the emptiness of life without him? Was she strong enough to risk it?

Cal could see the doubt and insecurity in Andrea's eyes. But until he fixed the other aspects of his life, his career, his…mind, he did not know what to say to reassure her. He no longer believed everything would be all right, he just didn't know anymore. Nor did he still believe he was absolutely the best thing for her, knowing he may soon be just a broken-down *former* fireman.

All he knew for certain, as he stared deep into her cinnamon-brown eyes, was that this woman was not only the love of his life, she was his anchor, the foundation of his future. And he had to hold it together a little longer…for her.

"How is he?" Marty asked quietly. Reaching forward, she used the wooden tongs to pick up a crescent roll.

"Okay, I guess," Andrea answered softly, neither woman wanting their private conversation to become public. She quickly glanced back over her shoulder at Cal, who was leaning against the wall on the opposite side of the room. She watched as one of their many friends approached him and shook his hand. The two men became engaged in conversation.

"Did he say anything more about the other night?"

"No." Andrea turned away when she felt herself blushing. She was only now considering that Marty may have heard their lovemaking. She shuffled forward as the buffet line moved along, surveying the offerings. But she wasn't thinking of the wide assortment of foods on display, only of the man who stood a short distance from her.

"Look, I don't know exactly why he was there the other night, but he needs to watch himself while he is on suspension. If someone else would've found him in there he could've got in a lot of trouble." Marty moved along the line close behind her, speaking close to her ear so no one else could hear.

Andrea's lips pulled into a flat line as she listened in strained silence. She loved Marty like a sister, but she knew in this particular battle Marty was firmly on Cal's side. Her anger stirred as she considered the fact that Marty was probably encouraging Cal to stay with the department.

Nothing had changed in the past week since she'd found Cal sleeping at the firehouse. He was still having nightmares, still doing everything in his power to return to the department, and still refusing to share anything of what he was going through with her. The stress of her life was becoming unbearable, something had to change. Andrea felt like a dry twig in a strong storm, certain that the next big gust of wind would be the one to break her.

She watched as Marty used another pair of tongs to sprinkle a heaping of salad on her plate, and continued moving, completely oblivious to Andrea's private contemplations. "That kind of strange behavior could affect his whole career, not to mention what the shrink would make of it. The department will never let him come back to work without a positive psyche eval. Just tell him to watch himself, we need him back as soon as possible."

Andrea slanted her friend a narrowed glance. "Since you are so concerned with his career, why don't you tell him yourself?" she spat, before turning and quickly walking away from Marty and the buffet table.

Marty stood with wide eyes and an open mouth, watching Andrea's retreating back.

Luckily, the conversation had not been loud enough for others to hear, so Marty continued to prepare her plate as if nothing had happened. She knew what was wrong. Andrea was afraid, and Marty knew the fear was not without credit. What they did was dangerous, and death was an accepted possibility. Still, she wondered how Cal was ever going to return to the life he loved if the woman he loved would not support his decision and his recovery? At the end of the day, Big Cal was a firefighter, and despite what Andrea believed, he would never be content behind a desk.

"Aren't you going to eat?" Andrea approached him, and offered the plate in her hand.

Cal shook his head slightly. "Maybe, later." He reached up and rubbed his forehead. "Just wish I could get rid of this damn headache."

Andrea knew the headache was due to a lack of sleep combined with intense stress. "I have an Advil in my purse." Even as she offered, Andrea already knew what the answer would be.

"You know I don't take medication."

"Cal, it's just a pain reliever."

"I said no!" He closed his eyes tightly.

When he opened them again, Andrea was glaring up at him, and he realized everyone in the hall was staring at them.

"I've had it," she whispered, and Cal could see the finality of the statement in her eyes. "I just can't do this anymore."

He knew she was going to run even before she turned away, but somehow he just could not bring his feet to move to stop her. Later he would reflect that some part of him did not want to stop her, the part of him that believed she deserved better than a piece of a man.

He watched as she hurried out of the room. Cal immediately dropped his head not wanting to deal with a room full of shocked expressions. His battered ego had had all the beating it could take. First his mind, then his job, and now his woman…there was nothing left.

Chapter 14

The two men sat with their heads together in earnest conversation, never noticing the attention they were garnering from every woman in the room. One was small, sleek, with the face of an angel, the other was not as handsome but attractive in his own way, his defining feature being large, rippling muscles that seemed to cover his whole body. The kind that made a woman want to run her hands over every inch of him to see if he was real. So different in appearance it would not occur to a casual observer that they may be related.

From the moment his little brother came into the world, Cal had to listen to exclamations regarding his looks. Everything from "Cal, isn't your little brother a beautiful baby?" That one came from his favorite aunt, Aunt Felicia. To girls in school accosting him in the halls for introductions. "Cal, why don't you hook me up with that fine brother of yours?" That one came from a cheerleader named Merika, a girl Cal had had a crush on for the first two years of middle school.

But despite all the adoration and praise his little brother got for his unusual good looks, Cal could never bring himself to resent Steve. Despite appearances, they were brothers in every sense of the word.

From the moment Steve could toddle around behind Cal, he'd followed his big brother everywhere. Most of his ideas and opinions had subconsciously been formed by that connection, and Cal soon learned that it was difficult to not like someone who worshipped the ground you walked on.

Now they were both men, and equal in their own right, living thousands of miles apart and seeing each other rarely. But at times like this, sitting together, discussing their lives over a beer in the pool hall, they were just two brothers, sharing their thoughts and dreams, hopes and fears, and leaning heavily on each other.

"So, what are you going to do? Cancel the wedding?"

Cal sat with the beer mug between his hands, frowning down into the amber liquid. "No."

Steve tilted his head. He did not want to state the most obvious, and worst possibility, but someone had to. "But, what if she doesn't show up next week? Shouldn't you warn people who may be traveling from out of town?" *Or out of the country?* Steve kept the sarcastic remark to himself. It was the last thing his brother needed now.

"She'll show."

Steve studied Cal's pensive expression, trying to determine if he really believed that the woman who'd walked out on her own wedding rehearsal dinner planned to show for the actual wedding, or if he was just in really deep denial, but said nothing.

"She will," Cal snapped, but it came out as more of a growl. He took a deep breath to regain control of his slipping temper.

Steve's eyebrows lifted. *But what if she doesn't?*

The two sat in brooding silence for a while, before a thought occurred to Cal. "When are you scheduled to return to Africa?" he asked, leaning back in his chair.

"I was actually considering extending my vacation."

"Great. I know Mama will be happy to hear that."

"Yeah." He glanced at his brother as he considered returning to the most pressing topic. He knew he would have to find a different approach, but one way or another there were decisions that had to be made.

"Have you talked to Andrea since last night?"

Cal sighed heavily. "No. I keep calling, but she won't answer her phone."

There was so much Steve wanted to ask. But his brother was a private man—he always had been. What he had to say he would get to in his own time and in his own way. Until then, all Steve could do was try to be supportive.

Thoughts of love and loss automatically drew his mind to the locket in his pocket. His hand subconsciously went to it. "Cal. What do you know about Candace Pippins?"

"Cavanaugh's cousin?" Cal glanced at his brother with a knowing expression. "Not much, other than the fact that she's *married,* and *has a kid.*"

Steve smiled. "It's all right man, no need for the warning, I know all that. I'm not trying to get with her. I was wondering more about her family."

"What about her family?"

"Where are her people from?"

"I think most of them are in Savannah, but they're Creole, so maybe…Louisiana originally. Not sure, exactly." Cal tilted his head to the side and looked up at his brother in concern. "Where's all this coming from?"

Steve thought in silence for a moment, not knowing how what he was about to say would be accepted. Then he reached into his shirt and pulled the locket over his shirt, reaching behind his neck he undid the clasp and handed it to his brother.

Cal opened the locket and noticed the resemblance right away. "Whoa. Who is this?"

"Don't know, just found it in an antique store a few years ago. According to the dealer, it is at least a hundred years old."

"Wow." Cal flipped the small locket over in his

hand, examining the intricately carved engravings. He turned it back over and looked at the picture of the woman inside once more. "I get why you're asking about Candace. This lady does look a lot like her." He looked at the picture once more. "Eerie."

"I know." He paused. "So much so I'm wondering if maybe she could be a distant relative."

Cal's eyes widened. "Hmm, I guess anything is possible." He handed the locket back to his brother. "Why don't you ask Cavanaugh, he'd probably know."

"Thanks, I'll do that. Wanna shoot some balls?" Steve nodded in the direction of an empty table.

Cal drank the last of his beer and nodded. "Why not."

Steve racked the balls and leaned across the table to take the first shot. He was trying to shoot the eight ball in the corner pocket but he missed. He turned to chalk his cue, waiting for Cal to take his shot, then noticed Cal had not moved from the other side of the table where he stood leaning on his stick.

"Cal?"

Cal snapped to attention hearing his name. "Oh,

sorry man." He moved around the table trying to find the right shot. He finally found it, and bent over the table to take it. He missed, as well.

When he stepped back Steve was watching his face. "What's Andrea's problem with you, anyway?" he asked quietly.

"Don't ask." Cal shook his head.

Steve bent forward to take his shot.

"She knew what I was when we met! How the hell can she use it as an excuse to break up with me a year later?" He huffed. "A week before our wedding!"

It seemed the dam had burst. Steve took his shot and managed to get the five ball in the side pocket. "If you ask me, I think she is just having last-minute jitters."

"Women don't have last-minute jitters, Steve, that's a guy thing."

"I'm just saying, like you said, she knew a year ago that you were a firefighter, so why is this an issue now?"

"It's not just my occupation," Cal said quietly, chalking his stick.

Steve stopped and studied his brother's face, and knew instantly what he was thinking. "You're still having those nightmares?"

Cal nodded.

"Cal, you know if you ever expect to return to active duty, you're going to have to open up to someone and talk about this."

Cal took his shot, and a stony silence fell over the pair. Steve said nothing more. His brother was a proud man.

Some fifteen minutes later, there were only three balls left on the table. Cal leaned his hip on the table and gently tapped his stick against the floor. "They are about Andrea."

"What?" Steve was so startled by his brother's comment that he missed the shot.

"The dreams, they are about Andrea."

A few minutes later they were back at the table, having given up on the game.

"Does she know?" Steve asked, leaning on his folded arms.

"Don't you get it, man? That's why I can't talk to her about it." Cal rubbed his large hand over his head. "I mean, when they were just about the fire, they were bad enough. But now…how do you tell the woman you love that every night when you close your eyes you see her dying, again and again?"

Steve touched his brother's arm to express his

understanding. Never had he imagined that this was what Cal was struggling with. "I understand why you don't want to tell her about that. But what choice do you have?"

Cal glanced at him. "None, which is why I'm not telling her."

"Cal, you don't want to lose her, and all she wants is for you to share your fears with her."

"Not this."

"Come on, Cal, think about it—"

Cal shot up out of his chair and dug into his pocket for his wallet. "Look, man, I appreciate you letting me bend your ear. And I appreciate your concern, but this time, little brother—" he tossed a handful of bills on the table "—you don't know what the hell you're talking about."

Andrea heard a sound and pressed the mute button on the remote. After a few seconds more, she realized it was the chain on her front door rattling back and forth. She sighed in resignation. She'd been expecting this visit.

Slowly she unbent her body from where she sat cross-legged in the middle of her bed and went into the living room.

The first thing she saw was a long, brown arm

in the partially opened entryway. Apparently, he'd used his key and unlocked her apartment door and found his entrance blocked by the chain. He was trying to twist his hand around in some sort of a contortionist movement to remove the security chain from the outside. She shook her head. Instead of calling out to her for help, this was his answer to the problem. Herein lay the crux of their problems: he would rather struggle alone than simply ask for help.

Andrea stood silently with her arms folded over her chest wondering how long he would attempt the futile action before finally giving up. She'd originally hooked the chain when she came in the night before fearing Cal would follow her home. Having only just made her decision, she knew she would not have been strong enough to stand against his big strong comforting arms and soft brown eyes if he'd come into the apartment using the key she'd given him.

There wouldn't have been any groundbreaking confessions or serious contemplation of their problems. Just wild, hot, animalistic lovemaking. Andrea didn't kid herself into believing anything else. She needed time and distance to organize her thoughts and consider her actions. She'd waited for hours but he didn't follow her home. Although her phone continually rang, she could see on the ID caller that it was primarily her parents and her girlfriends. Around midnight, she finally unplugged the phone, curled in a ball and cried herself to sleep.

When she awoke, in the light of day, she was forced to admit her behavior the previous night had been extreme, but now there was no digni- fied way to undo it. She'd stormed out of her own wedding rehearsal in front of all her family and friends. Unless she wanted to appear flaky and in- decisive, she was now forced to stand behind her position. She'd accidentally backed herself into a corner, and now the only way out was forward.

Andrea realized last night she'd taken their wedding hostage, and now Cal was here to hear her ransom demands. Even as she steeled herself for the task, some part of her was terrified that he would not be willing to pay the price neces- sary to win her heart.

Cal suddenly stopped pulling at the chain, when he sensed her presence on the other side of the door. The feeling was confirmed by the familiar scent of cologne that came through the crack in the door and drifted into his nose, sensual and arousing.

He pressed his head against the wood door, considering how this must look from her point of view. When he'd first decided to come here, he hadn't really taken the time to formulate a plan or consider what to say. He was flying on pure instinct, believing that if he could just get her in his arms he could convince her that she belonged with him. But when he found the door chained, something snapped inside him. Something about the small gesture seemed too final, too complete.

"When did you start putting the chain on the door?"

"Last night."

"What did I do to make you hate me so much?"

"I don't hate you!" She suddenly sounded much louder, and he realized she stepped closer to the door.

"Then why are you locking me out?"

"We need to talk."

"Okay, open the door and we can talk."

"No…if I open the door, you're going to try to confuse me with kisses."

He was silent for a long time. "*Confuse* you with kisses?"

"You know what I mean!"

"Open the door, Andrea."

"No."

He sighed in defeat. "All right, talk. Why did you run out on me last night?"

"I needed to get your attention."

He huffed. "Well, you definitely got it. Along with everyone in the wedding party and both our families. You've even gotten the attention of the hundred people we invited to the wedding next week."

"I'm not saying I don't want to go ahead with the wedding."

"Running out on the groom during the rehearsal dinner is usually a pretty good indication that the bride does not want to go through with the wedding."

"I knew you would take this out of context!" She pushed his arm back through the small opening and slammed the door shut.

"Andrea!" Cal banged on the door. "I'm sorry, I'm listening." He laid his head heavily against the door. The weight of the world had finally become too much. "It's just I'm angry." He closed his eyes and forced himself to accept the truth. "No. I'm mad as hell. You broke our deal."

"What deal?" Her soft voice was barely audible through the door.

"You knew when we met that I had a problem committing to relationships. Every time I trusted my heart to a woman, I ended up getting dumped on. I didn't want to keep going through that. Then you came along and made me believe…you made me think you would never do that to me. You said you'd marry me and stay with me forever. I believed you. But you didn't mean it." Cal heard the chain rattling and then the door was thrown open.

"How can you say that? I did mean it!"

Cal's eyes took in her tired form, and realized she hadn't slept any better than he had. She was still wearing her apricot dress from the night before. "Then how could you walk out on me in front of our family and friends?"

"I had to," she pleaded. "Don't you understand? If I don't take a stand now, I never will."

He looked down into her face twisted with worry and determination. "What exactly are you standing against?"

"You still don't understand." She shook her head slowly. "It's not what I'm standing against, Cal. It's what I'm standing for."

"And what's that?"

"The truth."

"What are you talking about? I've never lied to you."

"Maybe not with your mouth, but with your actions, your body language, and every time you shut yourself off from me. You tell me your heart is mine, then you hide it away from me. You say you want me to share your life but you won't tell me what is going on *in your life.*"

"Is this about the nightmares?"

"Partly, but so much more than that. This is about *real* commitment, this is about *true* devotion."

He shook his head in confusion. "Just tell me what you want, Andrea."

"I want you to trust me."

"I do trus—"

"No, you don't. If you did, I would know what images wake you up in a cold sweat. Why you feel the need to search through the firehouse files at two in the morning, why you froze in that house fire. These are the things you refuse to share with me. And quite honestly, I don't know if you can.

"So, there it is, Cal. What I want from you." She spread her arms wide in a gesture of a grand announcement. "I *challenge* you to *trust* me."

Cal took in her dramatic pose and could almost see the vein of steel running up her spine. There was no doubt about it, this was a make-or-break demand and he knew instantly that he could not do it. No hesitation, no uncertainty. No way he could accept her challenge.

Steve's words played over in his mind. *All she wants is for you to share your fears with her.* They both made it sound like such a simple request. Cal dropped his head, turned his back on the woman he loved and walked away.

Chapter 15

Cavanaugh stood on the porch waiting for someone to answer the door. Like most of the dinner guests of family and friends, he'd been left blowing in the wind the previous evening as they all watched Andrea run out of the restaurant. They all wanted to help the troubled couple, but nobody knew how.

This morning, a thought had occurred to him of how he could possibly help. He could at least close the case on Cal's questions regarding Jeff Collins once and for all.

Finally, the front door of the small house

opened, and Cavanaugh found himself wrapped in warm, loving arms. He accepted the older woman's strong embrace with patience. Evelyn Palmer held his slender body away from her and looked him over with the assessing eye of a mother. "Is Marty feeding you?" she asked with a bluntness only few people would ever try.

Cavanaugh sighed. "Yes, Evelyn, I eat very well. Is JJ around?"

Refusing to be so easily dissuaded, she completely ignored the question. "Not all that restaurant food, I mean real home-cooked meals."

He squeezed his way around her to avoid getting a doughnut stuck in his mouth, which was not an unrealistic possibility with Evelyn. Ever since the woman had met him, she'd been sticking unwanted food in his mouth. Her only criteria seemed to be the more fatty content the better. For some reason, she seemed to think that any man with less than a forty-two inch waist was malnourished.

Speaking of forty-two inch waist, Cavanaugh thought, as his friend JJ appeared in the doorway from the kitchen with an apple in his hand. "Hey, man, what's up." JJ motioned over his shoulder and then led the way up the stairs to the bedroom he used as a home office.

"Good seeing you." Cavanaugh gave Evelyn a quick kiss on the cheek and followed her husband up the stairs.

"Have you had lunch?" she called after the pair.

In unison, the men gave opposite answers. Cavanaugh answered in the affirmative, while his companion almost whined out *no*.

"You know the deal." Evelyn shook her finger at her husband. "You finish that apple and we'll discuss a pastrami sandwich later."

Cavanaugh followed into the office and sat down in an easy chair sitting in the corner. "So, what's with the apple?"

JJ's thick eyebrows scrunched in irritation. "High cholesterol. She's been making me add more fruits and vegetables to my diet. According to my doctor I eat too much meat, but my feeling is, if an all-meat diet is good enough for a lion, it's good enough for me."

"So she makes you eat an apple?"

JJ nodded.

"And rewards you with a pastrami sandwich?"

"Hey, man, marriage is all about compromise."

Cavanaugh laughed. "A lesson I'm learning more and more with each day."

JJ tossed the file through the air like a Frisbee

to his friend, and Cavanaugh caught it reflexively. "I think you and Cal may be barking up the wrong tree with this Jeff guy. From all accounts, he's just what he appears to be, a highly decorated officer of the Detroit fire department."

"You sure?" Cavanaugh asked, flipping through the pages. He knew the guy had to be clean to have been admitted to the academy, but he did think there would some departmental reprimands in his files, something to reflect questionable conduct. But as he glanced over the pages it became evident that as far as the department was concerned, as far as the world was concerned, Jeff Collins was a pretty decent guy.

Cavanaugh sighed and set the file down beside his chair. "Okay, so now we know what the record says, but I'm telling you, JJ, there is something not right about this dude."

"Be specific."

"I can't. I don't work with the guy, it's just a feeling I get when I'm around him. But Cal thinks the man wants him dead."

"Why? Have they had some sort of confrontation?"

"That's just it. They haven't. Cal is certain

they never met before Fifteen, but he says Jeff watches him like a hungry jackal."

JJ sat with one hip on his desk. "You can't exactly investigate dirty looks, Cavanaugh. If you really think this guy is up to something, we need more information."

"Can you tail him for a while? Maybe for a week, see where he goes, who he talks to."

JJ smiled remembering how they'd met. Marty had hired him to shadow Cavanaugh for his own protection, but unfortunately Cavanaugh realized he was being followed and turned the tables on both of them. "Sure. As long as he's not as sharp as you, that shouldn't be a problem."

Cavanaugh smiled in return. "Thanks, man." Once the business part of their meeting was concluded, the friends spent some time just catching up on each other's news.

During the previous years, the pair had spent quite a bit of time together while looking into the attempts on Cavanaugh's life. But since then, they'd not been able to see each other often, except for the occasional dinner outing, which usually included the wives.

About an hour later, Cavanaugh stood to leave. "Think I can sneak out the back door? I have a feeling Evelyn is probably guarding the front door with some kind of meat sandwich she'll want to shove down my throat."

"Probably." JJ chuckled, then his expression quickly became angry. "She better not try to give you my pastrami." He looked at Cavanaugh with consideration. "Yeah, we better take you out the back."

Cavanaugh laughed again and followed his friend out, realizing he'd just been outrated by a sandwich.

Andrea glanced at the red flashing button on her answering machine before grabbing her lunch bag out of the refrigerator. She didn't have time to return calls and assure everyone of her well-being—she was running late for work. Besides, she wasn't sure what she would tell them anyway. Should she call off the wedding? Should she just wait? There was still too much unsettled between them.

After Cal's visit the previous day, she'd spent most of the afternoon fighting herself, finally falling asleep early that morning. Every fifteen minutes or so she found herself headed in the direction of the phone. All she wanted to do was call

Cal and surrender, cry mercy, beg him to forget everything she'd said and please, please forgive her.

She'd reach out for the phone and then notice how much her trembling hands resembled her mother's and she would snatch it back. Of course, her situation in no way resembled the kind of marital discord her mother lived with. And there was never any question of Cal being like her father.

What she feared was that she had inherited the compromising nature of her mother. That something inside that refused to fight when the odds were stacked against her. It reeked of cowardice, and this was the fight of her life, not only for herself but for Cal, as well. She *could not* give up.

She grabbed a bagel out of the box on the table as she hurried toward the living room. Taking one final look around the room she swung open the door and stopped in her tracks.

Lying in the center of the welcome mat was a white envelope. Setting her purse and lunch bag down, she quickly opened it. Her breath caught in her throat when she found a picture of her and Cal cuddled together in a picture booth.

She remembered exactly when the photo had

been taken, shortly after they'd started dating.
She was so happy and excited about the budding
relationship. Now, that seemed so long ago. She
flipped the picture over and read the few scribbled words on the back.

*What we have is more than some people
will ever hope to have.*
I love you. That should be enough.

Andrea's eyes narrowed on the words, then
she quickly stuck the picture and envelope down
in her purse. *The man fights dirty,* she thought,
knowing Cal was trying to incite memories of
happier times. It worked.

But it changed nothing. The picture did invoke
happy memories, but it was of a time when they
meant little to each other. Now, even in this time
of trial, he was the sun and moon in her world.
Now…he meant everything.

She hurried down the hall toward the elevator.
If anything, seeing the picture had only strength-
ened her resolve.

Cal watched his friend moving toward him
across the crowded lobby. Cavanaugh reached

him with an extended arm, and the men shared the brief brotherly hug they always exchanged when meeting. "Sorry you had to come down here, man. But this week has been like a madhouse."

"No problem. I appreciate you doing this for me. And tell JJ thanks, too."

"Already have."

Cal looked down at the brown envelope Cavanaugh held in his hands. "Anything I should know about right away?"

"Not really. According to JJ, the guy is a real straight shooter. Nothing out of the ordinary in his jacket, a couple of speeding tickets. No reprimands in his department record, just commendations."

Cal frowned, wondering if his instincts were failing him for the first time. "Really, I was sure you would find something."

Cavanaugh glanced at his watch before continuing. "If it's any consolation, I'm with you. Something about the guy is not right, but so far there is nothing in his background that JJ could find to substantiate what we feel."

"Well, I just want to read through it anyway."

"I understand." Cavanaugh checked his watch again.

"Look, I don't want to hold you up, I know

you have to get back to your meeting, but thanks again, man. I really owe you one."

"No problem," Cavanaugh called over his shoulder, already in motion. He paused a few feet away and turned back toward Cal. "Have you talked to Andrea?"

Cal nodded. "I don't think it's going to work. I may have to call off the wedding."

Cavanaugh walked back across the space dividing them. "Look, I know it seems impossible right now, but you've got to hang in there." He tried to glance at his watch inconspicuously. "Remember last year when Marty wouldn't talk to me, wouldn't see me?"

Cal quirked an eyebrow with a smile. "I remember, you looked like a lost little puppy standing outside the firehouse." His smile turned into a frown. "It's not so funny when it's you."

"Yeah, well, back then I thought it was over. I thought I had lost her for good, but look at us now."

Cal tried to smile realizing his friend was trying to give him hope. "Thanks, man."

Cavanaugh nodded. "I've gotta go, but you hang in there. Don't give up." Then he was rushing across the lobby back the way he came.

Cal stood alone in the empty lobby. He flipped

open the brown envelope and glanced at the generic information. Cavanaugh was right; on paper, Jeff Collins was nothing less than an upstanding citizen and an outstanding firefighter. But paper did not feel, and Cal knew what he felt in the presence of Jeff was not comforting in the least.

He thought about Cavanaugh's words of encouragement, but Cavanaugh did not know about Andrea's challenge, or the PTSD. He didn't know the whole story. No one but he and Andrea knew what was really at stake. He knew Cavanaugh meant well, but the truth was he didn't understand. It was easy to be confident when you knew you could give your woman what she wanted.

Less than an hour later, he stood beside Marco's bed in his small bedroom, looking down into the young face so filled with indecision.

He hated asking the question, but knew he must. They had to put a stop to this potential killer right away.

"Marco, did you see anything or anyone else in the building?"

The young man's eyes darted nervously in every direction as he struggled to find a way to avoid answering the question.

But it was too late; Cal had already seen the memory reflected on his face. "Marco, you saw who started the fire, didn't you?"

Big brown eyes darted across his face and returned to the sheet as he struggled his thin shoulders. "I don't know, maybe." He glanced at his mother standing on the other side of the bed. "I think so."

Maria leaned across the bed. "Marco, if you saw something—anything—you have to tell us. This is a very bad person, and he is trying to hurt people. Do you understand?"

Marco nodded, his dark brows crunched in concern. "But what if he finds out it was me who told on him?"

Cal fought to hide the surprise he was suddenly feeling. "What are you saying, Marco? Do you know this person? Have you seen them before?"

He nodded slowly. "Yes, at the firehouse."

Cal and Maria exchanged a startled glance.

Cal had a sinking feeling in the pit of his stomach, and a fairly good idea of the man Marco was about to name. Although he'd already had his own suspicions, still he had not wanted to believe that a firefighter could turn into an arsonist. It was crazy to imagine that someone who fought the monster everyday and saw the damage that it could do would be the very person who could cause such destruction.

"Who did you see?" he asked the question with a heavy heart, despite his certainty he still needed for Marco to name the man.

Marco bit his bottom lip once more, still unsure if he should confess. "You sure he won't find out?" He looked up at his friend and hero. "He's not like you, Cal. He's mean."

Cal reached across the bed and took the tiny hand in his much larger one. "Marco, I promise you, as long as I'm alive, no one will hurt you."

Marco looked to his mother for courage and she nodded with a smile.

"It was the new guy. He poured gasoline on everything then threw down a match and ran out of the room. I saw him as he ran past me."

Cal felt his gut clinch and reflexively squeezed the little hand he was holding. He did not realize he'd done it until Marco flinched and pulled his hand away. Some part of his mind knew he should've apologized but he was too busy reeling from the bomb that had just been dropped.

It was true. Jeff Collins was the arsonist. The

man he'd brought into their firehouse, into their lives had destroyed several businesses and almost took a life. Just like he knew instinctively that Jeff was the guy, Cal also knew that he was the reason, although he wasn't certain exactly why. He knew somehow this was all about him.

Now, he had to find out why and put a stop to it before the man actually succeeded in hurting someone else, or worse, killing someone.

"Cal?" Marco's eyes widened in alarm. "Cal, you believe me, don't you?"

Cal allowed himself to be pulled out of his own private contemplations seeing the need for reassurance on his young friend's face. "Yeah, man, I believe you." He ran his large hand over the boy's short, curly hair. "Don't worry, little man, I'll stop him."

Cal's eyes met Maria's over the top of her son's head, and the message that was written there was clear. *How?*

"I need to get back to the firehouse, but I'll be back later, okay?" He tried to ignore the fear in Marco's eyes. He knew the boy wanted him to stay by his bedside, but he had an arsonist to catch.

"You promise you'll be back later?"

"Promise."

"Can you bring me a Butterfinger?" he asked hopefully, his brown eyes sparkling with anticipation.

Cal chuckled. "We'll see." As he started for the door, he heard Maria telling her son she would be right back and then Cal realized she'd followed him out into the hall.

"Cal, what do you plan to do?"

"First and foremost, I need to find Jeff Collins."

"Shouldn't you just leave this to the police?"

Looking into eyes so like her son's, Cal realized Marco wasn't the only one worried. "I will, but first I want to talk to him myself."

"Why?" She shook her head in confusion. "This man is dangerous."

"I'll be careful, Maria. Don't worry." He tried to smile to hide the doubt he was feeling, but was unsure how successful he was in convincing the woman.

A few minutes later as he rode the elevator down, Cal allowed himself to give in to his own fear and doubt.

The thought that he'd been sharing living quarters with a man who held some kind of grudge against him was one thing, but living with an arsonist was quite another. He'd almost killed an innocent child.

Despite what Maria believed, Cal knew it wasn't as easy as going to the police and letting them handle it. Jeff Collins was a decorated veteran firefighter whose whole life was about to be turned upside down on the word of a child.

The police, the fire marshal, they would all require something Cal just did not have: proof. Or at the very least, motive. Cal didn't have either, other than the thin memory of seeing him with the can of accelerant hidden under his arm. In fact, under different circumstances he would've been one of the greatest skeptics. It just didn't make any sense. But he'd take what he had to Mack, and let him make the decision.

Jeff Collins was definitely guilty of something, he thought while climbing into his truck. But was it arson?

Jeff was sitting in the common area when they came through the door. He looked up and knew that something was terribly wrong. The District chief, Mack, was in the lead. Followed by Cal, who was glaring at him like an angry bull, which in itself wouldn't have been cause for great alarm. But that inspector friend of his, Noel, was walking by his side, watching him with a kind of intensity. Not anger or malice, but definitely nothing good.

Those two were followed by two fully uniformed police officers. When the entourage stopped in front of his chair, Jeff stood. "What can I do for you?"

"Jeffrey Collins, you are under arrest for arson."

"What?" Jeff looked at each individual face wondering if this was some kind of crazy joke. "What are you talking about? I'm no arsonist!" Jeff only half heard his rights being read and then suddenly he was being pushed across the floor. He glanced back at Cal, knowing in his gut that he was the one responsible for all this. "First you steal my job, now my career!"

"What the hell are you talking about?" Cal knew he shouldn't have responded, but the accusation was so absurd he couldn't stop himself.

"I should've been the next chief—not you!"

Cal shook his head in disbelief. "Are you telling me that you did all this because you felt slighted over a promotion?"

A flash of confusion showed in Jeff's eyes

but quickly vanished. "Damn right! It should've been me!"

One of the two uniformed officers stepped forward. "Please place your hands behind your back." Without waiting for compliance, the officer pulled Jeff's arms behind him and placed the handcuffs on.

"I'm going to get you for this, Brown!" he vowed as he was guided through the door. "You're not going to get away with this!"

As he was shoved into the police car with all his team members looking on in amazement, Jeff was already working on his plot for revenge. He'd tried to do things by the book, tried to bring the man down by legitimate means. But obviously Cal Brown wasn't going to play by the rules...so neither would he.

Chapter 16

Marianne sat beside Andrea at her small dining table, feeling like a complete sellout and traitor. She listened as Andrea went through the list of all the things necessary to undo six months of planning. She nodded at the appropriate time and pretended to take notes. Secretly, she had no intention of undoing anything.

She'd received a call yesterday afternoon from Cal stating that in no uncertain terms was she to cancel any part of their wedding preparations. She'd started to protest—after all, Andrea was her client—until Cal gave her indisputable evi-

dence of his love for his fiancée. He offered
Marianne a bribe—a rather nice one at that.

But the money was not why she'd chosen to
do it. Truth of the matter was that despite her
many years of planning weddings, half of which
had ended in divorce, Marianne was still very
much a romantic. She decided any man willing
to bribe his wedding planner to keep his wedding
from being canceled deserved a second chance.

Using a pen, Andrea ran down the list of items
on the notebook in front of her. "Okay, I think
that is everything." She ripped it off and handed
it to Marianne. "I'm sorry about all this, Marianne."

Marianne forced a smile. "No problem." She
looked at the troubled face of the pretty young
woman she'd been working so closely with for
six months. *I hope I'm doing the right thing.*

"Here's the list of our guests." She started to
hand over the neatly typed list of names and
phone numbers, and paused. "Never mind. I want
to call everyone myself."

"No!" Marianne sealed her lips tightly when
she realized she'd shouted. She was quickly realizing that she was not cut out to be a double
agent. "Um, you have so much on your mind

right now, Andrea. Let me do this for you." She reached across the table and covered Andrea's hand. "I want to help in any way I can."

Andrea gave her a strange look and smiled. "Are you sure?"

Not trusting her own voice, Marianne just nodded and hid her sigh of relief when Andrea handed over the list. She glanced down at the information in her hand, certain that she had gotten all the important lists away from Andrea.

She stood, eager to be away from the scene of the crime. "All right, then, I'll be going. I've got lots to do, lots to do." She pushed her large glasses up on her nose and grabbed up her attaché. "I'll call you later."

Andrea stood watching her. "Marianne, is everything okay?"

"Oh yes, just fine." She hurried across the room and out the door. "Bye, bye," she called just before the door slammed behind her.

Soft, warm lips pressed gently against her mouth as a large, calloused hand outlined her breast beneath her thin, silk gown. Her lips puckered in expectation of the kiss that soon came. Her back arched seeking to fill his hand,

and she groaned in pleasure and anticipation. Knowing instinctively who covered her, Andrea wrapped her arms around the familiar hard body feeling his warm breath on her breast.

His broad shoulders felt so good and solid under her fingers. She felt his thigh between her legs gently pushing them apart. The cool air hit her hot center and triggered an alarm.

The heavy weight pinning her to the bed, the moisture forming between her legs, it all seemed so strangely real.

"Cal?" She whispered the word, even as she turned her head to the side to give him better assess to her neck.

Cal took the invitation, kissing a path along her soft skin. "Shh, it's okay, baby, I've got you."

Her legs lifted of their own accord to wrap around his waist as her mind tried to understand the situation. She finally opened her eyes and focused on the bedside clock. It was almost three in the morning. Her head fell back as she felt the coarse jean material pushing against her center.

Cal wrapped his hands around her bottom, pressing her up against him. "I've missed you so much." He whispered in her ear while fumbling with his button fly. "I've been going crazy without you."

Andrea was caught somewhere between ultimate pleasure and complete confusion. Taking Cal's face between her hands, she looked directly in his eyes. Even in the dark room she could see the sparkle of lust and triumph there.

"What are you doing?" She pushed at his chest but he didn't bulge. In a fit of rage, she slapped him. "How dare you! Get up!" she growled.

Cal stared down at her for a moment more before rolling over onto his back and away from her. "Your body is saying you missed me as much as I missed you, so why are you fighting me?"

She scooted to a sitting position. "You can't do this, Cal! You can't just come in here in the middle of the night and climb into bed with me like it's no big deal!"

He sat up on his elbows. "You never minded before."

"We are not together anymore."

"Who says?"

Her eyes widened in amazement. "I say!"

He pointed an index finger at her. "No, you said we weren't going to get married until I accepted your challenge. You never said anything about being broken up."

She shook her head frantically. He was twisting everything around. She sat up on her knees, and reached over to turn on the lamp on her bedside table. "The two things go hand in hand and you know it!"

Cal's hungry eyes quickly ran up her exposed thigh and over every inch of exposed skin. It didn't take much imagination to remember what was beneath the beige silk gown. "Andrea...do you still love me?"

There he goes playing dirty again. "What does that have to do with anything?"

"That has everything to do with everything."

Andrea ran both her hands over her tired eyes. "Go home, Cal."

His eyes narrowed in silent challenge. "I am home. You're my home."

The words were spoken with such conviction, she felt her whole insides melting. How easy it would be to give in to him. She allowed herself one quick glance over his prone form. Just a little treat, but it was too much. In his aroused state, with those all-knowing eyes watching her, he was far too much temptation.

"No, Cal, if I were your home you would feel comfortable with me. You would sha—"

"Hell." With one push he was off the bed. "Never mind." He grabbed his shirt off the floor where he'd apparently discarded it and began pulling it over his head. "You won't win this, Andrea. So you might as well give it up now. I love you, but I can't give you what you want. You're going to have to let it go."

"I can't."

He bent forward and braced his fists on the end of the bed. "Just tell me this. Why did you wait until within days of our wedding to have this little crisis?"

Little crisis? "Get out!"

"Not until you answer the question."

Andrea considered not answering for several long moments, before finally responding. "Because, as much as I love you, as much as I desire you, I couldn't accept the truth. I kept wishing, hoping you would let me in, but you wouldn't. You won't ever. I finally understand that."

"Understand this! In four days we *are* getting married, even if I have to drag you down the aisle!"

"I sat down with Marianne today. She is already in the process of canceling—"

"Hah! Wrong!" he said with a wicked chuckle.

Andrea drew back at his bold statement. Her brows crunched in confusion as she watched him come toward her. He seemed so sure of himself, so much like the man she remembered.

With three long strides he came around to the side of the bed, and before she realized what was happening, he had Andrea wrapped in his arms. "I'll admit, I'm dealing with some things, and no, I'm not very good at sharing my problems. There are days when I feel as if I'm losing my mind, and before it's all said and done I may have to give up the job I love. I don't know what tomorrow will bring. But one thing is for certain, Andrea. I'm not giving you up."

Later that same day, Andrea pulled up in front of her family home and sat watching her mother consult the gardener as to the care and pruning of her precious rose bushes. Andrea did not recognize the man, so assumed he was probably new.

She watched as her mother pointed to a bush on the far side of the garden, the man standing with her nodded his head in understanding. It was strange how easily her mother took control of the care and protection of her garden and home, and yet had so little control over her own existence.

She had not spoken to her parents since the night of the rehearsal dinner, and only some deep-rooted sense of duty had brought her here now. She had no desire to be berated by her mother regarding her embarrassing behavior, and had no idea of how her father would react.

She sighed and opened her car door, deciding it was best just to get it over with. She came up behind the pair of heads together both pointing and nodding in the direction of the trellis of white roses that leaned against the house.

"Hi, Mom," she said softly, and was surprised when her mother turned in her direction with a full smile on her face.

"Hi, honey." Margaret quickly dismissed the gardener, leaving him to carry out her instruction. "How are you doing?" she asked, taking Andrea's arm in hers and guiding her toward the walkway leading to the side entrance.

Andrea looked into eyes so like hers and didn't know what to make of the soft concern she found there. She'd expected anger, disappointment, but not this. "I'm fine."

Soon she was seated at the table, and her

mother was preparing a pot of coffee. Andrea watched her in silence realizing for the first time that their little talks over coffee had become a ritual.

"Have you spoken to Cal since the other night?" Margaret asked softly as she filled the carafe with water.

Andrea's frown deepened. *What is going on here?* "Um, yes, we've spoken."

"And?"

"And...and he understands what it will take for me to marry him."

"Andrea," Margaret said with an exaggerated drawl as she turned to face her daughter. "Your father and I were talking."

Oh no.

"We were thinking that maybe this isn't such a bad thing."

Andrea just sat staring at her mother in confusion. "You and Daddy decided this, did you?"

"You're obviously having doubts about whether or not you're in love—"

"No, Mom, there are no doubts about whether or not I love him. We just need to work out the details of our life together before it's too late."

"Well, whatever your reasons, they are your

own. The point is, we were thinking that maybe you should come with us to Brazil."

"Brazil?"

Her mother smiled with pure pleasure. "Didn't I tell you? That was my final destination choice. We are going to immerse ourselves in their rich Afro-centric culture!"

Andrea chuckled, pleased to see her mother so excited about something. "If you say so."

Margaret reached across the table and took her daughter's hand. "Come with us, Andrea! You'll love it, and it will give you some time to clear your head and find out what you really want."

I already know what I really want. "Thanks, but I'm going to pass this time."

"Why? So you can sit around mooning by yourself? Believe me, feeling sorry for yourself solves nothing."

Before she could respond, Andrea heard her father enter the house. Her instinctively reaction was disbelief that she'd once again lost track of the time. In the next instant, she was on her feet and preparing to leave.

"I'd better get going." She came around the table and hugged her mother tightly.

"Hi, kitten." Her father came into the kitchen reading the mail he'd brought in. The mail she and her mother had never been allowed to bring in. Another one of his rules.

"Hi, Daddy."

His watchful eyes scanned the kitchen quickly before landing on his daughter. "Did your mother tell you about the trip?" He shook his head. "Brazil, of all places, but it's her trip."

"Yes, she did. Thanks, but I don't think that's such a good idea."

He continued to scan the mail. "Why not?"

He hadn't raised his voice even a little, but Andrea felt the tension level in the room rise instantly. Even her mother seemed suddenly more alert.

Andrea swallowed hard and continued. "I just don't think it would be a wise decision to take off for parts unknown right now."

"Who says right now? We won't be leaving for two weeks. And there are no parts unknown, we are staying in a five-star resort in Brasilia."

"Really I appreciate the offer, Daddy, but I just don't think—"

"That's the problem, Andrea! You don't think!"

Despite her best effort, Andrea jumped in fear. She found herself backing away from him and preparing to flee out the back door if necessary.

Andrew's eyes darted from his daughter to the back door as if he clearly read her intention. He sighed heavily. "All I'm saying is, look at the mess you made of this whole wedding fiasco. All because you did not give yourself enough time to get to know this guy. Now, all the family and friends we've invited from out of town, not to mention Cal's family, have to make last-minute cancellation plans. All because you acted rashly."

Andrea's eyes narrowed on his face. Her fear had vanished and been replaced by anger. "I did not act rashly. I love Cal. I apologize for the confusion over the wedding, but it wasn't because I didn't think things through." Andrea stood her ground, even when she noticed her fathers jawbone flexing. She expected him to lash out at any moment, but she'd determined long ago that if this day ever came, it would end a lot different than he expected.

His assessing eyes ran over her once more, and then he returned to his mail as he dismissed her out of hand. He turned and walked back into the other room.

Realizing she'd won the battle, but wise

enough not to stick around, Andrea quickly kissed her mother on the cheek, and headed toward the front entrance, knowing it was the quickest route to her car.

Her father appeared in the entryway again, blocking her path. "Maggie, where is my dry cleaning?" He leaned around Andrea to look at his wife. "I didn't see it hanging in the front closet. Didn't I ask you to pick it up today?"

Andrea heard her mother gasp in alarm. "Oh, Andrew, I had so much to do today it completely slipped my mind. I'll get it first thing in the morning."

"But there was a suit in there I wanted to wear to a client meeting tomorrow. First thing in the morning will be too late." He snarled between his teeth. "Go right now."

"But they're already closed." Her mother whimpered, glancing at the clock on the wall to be sure. "They closed at five."

"I give you one simple task in a ten-hour period and you cannot even get that done," he growled. "So what am I supposed to wear to my meeting?"

"I'm sure there is something appropriate in your closet."

Her father became completely still, and Andrea could feel the hairs on the back of her neck stand up. She suddenly realized it wasn't her father's ranting and raving that always forewarned that something terrible was about to happen. It was that sudden calm that would come over him, like now.

Like a wild animal conditioned to recognize danger, she knew what was about to happen. She hurried toward the doorway, and as she moved past her father, he dropped a petal light kiss on her forehead. "That's it, run along, kitten. I need to speak to your mother in private."

In that instant, Andrea hated herself, realizing she'd been as conditioned as her mother. Her mother would shriek in terror and she would run and hide. That's the way it had always been. The few times she'd broken the pattern, there had been dire consequences.

She was almost to the front door when she heard her mother's cry.

"Andrew, no!"

Unable to stop herself, Andrea turned and raced back to the kitchen. So many times she'd done this and regretted it until she said she would no longer interfere. Still her feet moved in the direction of the commotion, she was unsure what she would do once she got there, but she had to do something. *This madness has got to stop.*

"Stop it!" She rushed across the room without thought. "Stop it." She grabbed hold of her father's thick arm.

Her father swung around with a look of stunned surprise. "Just what the hell do you think you are doing?" He shook her loose easily.

"No!" Andrea raged with the fury of thirty years of helplessness. "No more! You won't hit her anymore!"

Margaret pushed her way in front of her husband to get between the two people she loved most in the world. "Andrea, just go," she whispered.

"No, Mom." Andrea did not realize she was crying until she felt the first salty tear fall into her open mouth. "No, I won't leave without you."

"Just who the hell do you think you are dealing with, young lady." By then, Andrew had regained his composure and tried to regain his viselike grip on his family.

"A man—just a man." Andrea felt the shaking all the way to her toes. This was her father, the man who'd ruled her world all her life. But it was time for him to give up the reins whether he liked it or not, and the first step in that was to get her mother out of the house. She couldn't think beyond that. And at the moment, that task in itself seemed almost monumental.

Andrew's dark eyes narrowed on her face. "I'm your father, Andrea Nicole. And you *will* treat me with all due respect!"

Andrea reached forward and grabbed her mother's arm, jerking her to stand behind her. "Well, with *all due respect,* Daddy, you will keep your hands off my mother!"

"Andrea, don't do this." Margaret's troubled eyes darted between her husband and her child. "Please, this is none of your concern! I'm begging you to just go, leave. Before it's too late."

"Too late for what?" She hissed the question, never taking her eyes off her father who was now trembling with rage. "I'm already two broken arms, seven broken ribs, one black eye and eight busted lips too late!"

Andrew's eyes widened in amazement.

"Oh my God! You've been keeping track!" Margaret pulled away from her daughter and covered her mouth with both her hands.

"Get out!" Andrew roared. "Get out of my house, and don't ever come back here."

Andrea ignored him and turned to face her mother. "Every time he hit you Mom, I felt it!" She pointed an accusing finger, as the tears continued to stream down her face. "Every single time, you never fought back! Every single time you made excuses for him!"

So caught up in her anguish, she never saw the attack coming, as her father made a slashing motion and clipped her across her ear. Andrea fell to her knees in pain, staring up at her father with pure hatred in her eyes.

He came to stand over her prone form with his hands fisted at his sides. "I said, get out of my house!"

Andrea's water-filled eyes narrowed as she imagined all the ways she could kill him. Without a word, she stood. As she slowly rose, she realized this was the first time her father had ever hit her, his rage had always been directed at her mother. But not anymore, she'd crossed the line and whatever amnesty she may have had while she'd turned a blind eye no longer existed. Whatever fragile bond they had was now completely severed.

She dusted herself off and turned toward her mother. "I'm leaving now, Mom. Are you coming with me?"

Margaret looked at her daughter with anger. "What are you asking me to do Andrea? Leave my husband? For what? Why? Where am I supposed to go? What am I supposed to do?"

Andrea glanced back at her father who stood stone-still with his hands fisted at his side, waiting with complete confidence in the outcome of this little discussion. He already knew what Andrea was only now realizing. Her mother had no desire to leave him, ever. Andrea herself had offered her ample ways and means of escape.

From the moment she'd gone off to college all those years ago, until his very moment, she'd stood both mentally and physically with her hand open, begging her mother to come with her. But now she understood, the blame could not be completely laid at her father's door…her mother had a hand in her own suffering. Her dysfunctional childhood was their *shared* responsibility.

Andrea looked from one to the other, two lost souls locked in an endless battle and neither wanting it to end. She refused to be a part of it anymore. Without another word, she turned and walked out of her parents' home, knowing she would never return.

Without thought, she started her car and as if

on autopilot she headed in the direction of the apartment complex near downtown. There was only one place she wanted to be right now, only one person she could go to. And despite everything that had happened in the last few days, she knew he would not turn her away.

Chapter 17

Cal stood in the open door of his apartment, waiting while Andrea stepped off the elevator. He'd been standing there from the moment he buzzed her into the building. He was trying desperately not to get his hopes up—after all, this little visit could mean almost anything. She could be just dropping off the stuff he'd left at her apartment for all he knew.

When the elevator bell rang and the doors began to open, Andrea stood alone in the middle of the elevator. Her troubled eyes came up to meet his.

He moved forward and wrapped her in his arms. "Andrea, what's wrong?"

She shook her head against his chest, wrapping her arms tightly around his waist, needing the warmth and comfort she knew she could only find with him. "I just came from my parents'."

He nodded in understanding. He shifted his arm to her shoulders and guided her into the apartment. "What happened?"

Andrea went willingly to the couch. "I finally accepted that my mother doesn't want to leave him."

Cal sat down beside her and turned to face her, taking both her hands in his much larger ones. "Baby, I told you that a long time ago."

"I know, it's just I always thought, maybe she just wasn't strong enough, maybe she needed someone to encourage and support her."

"Some women do, but then again, there are some who don't want to be helped."

"Like my mother." Andrea added the part of the statement she knew he'd intentionally left off.

"Like your mother," he confirmed. "Are you okay?"

"I will be." She glanced at him. "I just didn't

want to be alone right now. I hope it was okay coming here."

He lifted her chin, resisting the urge to kiss her. "You will always be welcomed here."

She studied his brown eyes, trying to see past the surface. "Even though I kicked you out of my bed last night?"

"No matter what happens, Andrea, we will always be friends."

"I still love you," she whispered the words, knowing in her heart how unfair it was to say it, when she was the one who walked away.

"I never doubted it." He smiled and lifted her hand to his lips for a gentle kiss. "But as you said, not enough to be my widow. And I can't say that will never happen. Andrea, we both knew the risks of what I do. Every time the call comes, you just never know."

"Sure you wouldn't consider being a short order cook? Or maybe a florist?" Although there was a certain true desire to the words, the playful twinkle in her eyes belied any seriousness.

"Oh no." He frowned. "Haven't you read the statistics on short order cook burns? It's damn near an epidemic. And don't even get me started on the dangers of pruning roses. I get chills just thinking about it."

Andrea smiled. "See, I knew you would make me feel better." She reached up to give him a brief, friendly hug and found herself locked in a tight embrace. When she tried to pull back, she felt Cal's mouth covering hers, and her body being pressed back into the couch. In an instant, he was over her, urgently grinding against her crotch.

She pushed playfully at his shoulders, squirming to get free of him. "What are you doing?"

He quirked an eyebrow and gently rotated his hips against her. "Don't tell me it's been so long you don't remember this?"

She laughed. "I remember enough to know we are not supposed to be doing it. Friends, remember?" She pushed against him again, and he begrudgingly lifted his heavy weight off of her.

"I'm okay with friendship sex." His hungry eyes took her voluptuous curves.

Andrea sat up and just for safe measure scooted back toward the opposite end of the couch. "What exactly is friendship sex?"

"When two friends get together for completely meaningless sex. No strings attached." He grinned wickedly, and she was unable to do anything but smile in return seeing the mischievous glint in his soft brown eyes.

"Where I come from, they call that a booty call."

He hunched his shoulders. "Whatever. So, are you up for it?"

She laughed openly at the eager expression on his face. "Of course not!"

He feigned an exasperated sigh. "Well, I'm out of ideas. So, what do you want to do?"

She looked toward his kitchen. "How about I make up a batch of my world-class margaritas and you order a pizza." Seeing the puzzled expression on his face, her heart sank. "Unless you threw out all the margarita makings when I left." Andrea knew she was really asking if he'd thrown out all signs of her presence in his small apartment and had begun to move on.

"It's only been a few days, Andrea." He smiled, hearing the insecurity in her voice. "Everything is just as you left it. It's just I was thinking after an evening of pizza and margaritas I'm going to want some—"

"Don't even say it." She laughed, and headed toward the kitchen.

"Friendship sex!" he called after her.

* * *

Two hours, two pizzas and three margaritas each later, they both sat cross-legged on opposite sides of the living-room coffee table.

Cal was bare from his waist up, but Andrea was down to her bra and panties and from the look of the hand she was holding, something else was about to come off. She glared at Cal across the deck of cards. "Hit me."

Cal reached forward and laid the top card facedown in front of her. His eyes drifted down to her exposed cleavage and he subconsciously licked his lips.

Andrea picked up the card and cursing tossed it back. "I think you are cheating."

Cal picked up his own card and tossed it back. "Nope, just focused."

"We've played poker a hundred times, and you've never played this well."

His hungry eyes darted back to her breasts before he refocused on the cards in his hand. "Never had this kind of motivation."

"Hit me," she said again, and Cal gave her another card. She smiled and tucked it neatly in her hand, before tossing away a three of hearts.

Cal saw the triumphant expression pass over

her face before she quickly hid it. "Don't get smug now, all I need is two more wins and I'll have you just where I want you." He pulled a card and tossed it back, before continuing. "Bare as a baby."

"Well, don't get your hopes up too high. I'm not naked just yet." She spread her hand across the table and it was a full house. "Take that!"

Cal tossed down his own hand in defeat. "Damn! So close!" He began to reshuffle the cards.

Andrea stood and stretched, then reached for her blue jeans.

Cal looked up at the rustling sound. "Where are you going?"

"Home. It's getting late and I have an early shift tomorrow." She winked. "I have to sleep off these margaritas. And if I remember right, you start a new cycle in the morning."

He made a noise that sounded strangely close to a whine. "Come on, two more hands." He thought about how close he'd come to getting her panties off, it was like being within reach of the finish line and suddenly finding yourself yanked back to the starting gate.

Andrea smiled in a way that said she knew exactly what he was thinking. "Sorry to disappoint you, my love, but you won't be seeing these," she pointed to her breasts, "anytime soon."

"We'll see," he grumbled under his breath, and began collecting up the cards. Once she was fully dressed, Andrea came around to where he still sat like a moping child. "Thank you," she whispered with a soft kiss on his cheek. "For everything."

The sad expression gave way to a soft smile. "Anytime."

As Andrea let herself out of the apartment, he continued to sit at the table playing solitaire and trying not to notice how empty the apartment suddenly seemed. Cal was convinced that Andrea just needed some time. But the wait was killing him.

Twenty minutes later, he was just putting the cards back in the box and preparing to head to bed early. Sometimes when Andrea was heavy on his mind, sleep would help chase her away…for a while. The phone rang and he answered without looking at the ID caller.

"Is the offer for friendship sex still on the table?"

Cal smiled. "On the table, the chair, the bed, anywhere you want it."

The knock came on the door instantly, and he crossed the room quickly to open it. She stood there like a dejected doll, her shoulders slumped, her head bowed and all he wanted to do was pick her up in his arms, carry to his bed, and kiss away the heartache.

Giving in to impulse, he swooped her up in his arms and Andrea's arm came around his neck without hesitation.

"I don't know if this is such a good idea. I'm suppose to be getting over you," she whispered against his neck.

He kissed her forehead. "Trust me, this is the best idea you've come up with in days." He leaned back to look down in her face, as his own spread in a wicked smile. "And as for the other, that's fine, too. You know I like to be on top. But if *you want to get over me,* I'm okay with that."

She laughed and pushed against him. From her position cradled in his arm the motion was barely felt. "That's not what I meant."

Andrea continued to hold tight as he lowered her to the bed. She couldn't seem to let go. She hadn't felt this safe, *this right,* in days.

When she felt his soft lips touch hers, suddenly nothing else mattered except opening her mouth and welcoming his warm tongue. Her fingers wound their way through his tight curls as she pressed his head to hers needing to savor every drop of his sweet taste.

She couldn't stop herself from touching him. His thick arms, muscled shoulders, her eager fingers roamed over every inch of skin she could reach refamiliarizing herself with the body she loved almost as much as the man. It seemed like it had been months since she'd felt his heavy weight bearing her into a mattress, when in truth it had only been a few days.

The need was an all-consuming thing taking her over, and Andrea was certain she would die from pure want. She felt the slight pressure of a warm palm pressing against her inner thigh and her legs immediately fell open to welcome him home.

Without hesitation, Cal settled himself against her center and took her face between his hands. "I love you, Andrea." He looked directly into her eyes so that she could see the truth of his words. There was no way he could love her and not have her understand the truth of it. There could never be anything casual and friendly in what they shared.

The fierceness in his brown eyes took her breath

away. She swallowed hard and blinked once, but could not seem to speak, not that she needed to speak.

He'd laid his claim. She now knew the rules of this game. Rule number one being…this was no game.

Cal rose above her and covered her body with his, and she parted her rosebud mouth to welcome him, even as her arms snaked around his neck to pull him closer. Cupping her small bottom in his large hands he pressed her center against the coarse material of his jeans. Gently grinding against her soft core with the promise of what was to come.

Andrea's head fell back in surrender as the warm moisture rushed down in respond to her lover's silent call. She lay cradled in his arms like a rubber doll, completely satisfied to be vulnerable to his every whim. His calloused palm slowly ran over every inch of her skin, caressing and stroking, rolling and rubbing until Andrea could hardly breathe for her pounding heart. Her nails clawed at his shoulders when he pulled away to undress, but within moments he was back in her arms.

She felt the latex-covered knob pushing at her center, and she struggled to hold on in the whirlpool that threatened to sweep her away. "Oh, Cal." Unable to say any more, Andrea lifted her body and parted her legs wider.

She reveled in his hot breath on her neck, her breast, his heart pounding against hers. No matter how many times they made love it was always, always this good. Even with everything so wrong between them, he still felt like everything was right.

"I love, you, Cal," she moaned on a half breath as his thickness slid deep inside her body. "I will always love you."

"Shh," he cooed lovingly, before reaching around to cup her bottom in his strong hands. Slowly, carefully, he rocked in and out of her body until she thought she would go insane with the wonderful feeling of him.

"Don't stop." Andrea clung to him, feeling the heat build and build until she thought she would be consumed by the flames.

"I won't," he groaned against her skin.

"Please." In that moment, the truth of everything became completely clear to her. Just as she knew she was about to reach the top of the mountain, she knew as certainly that Cal was the only man who could ever take her there.

"I won't."

For one brief moment, before her whole body went up in flames fate gave Andrea a glimpse of her life without Cal. But the image had no time to fester her feeling of satisfaction because soon Cal was burning with her.

She threw back her head and cried out in both pleasure and pain.

When Andrea opened her eyes some time later, she found herself still cocooned in a blanket of warmth and peace. She yawned and attempted to stretch but was restricted by Cal's tight hold. She had no great desire to get free of his hold, so instead she snuggled closer to his chest.

What a fool I am, she thought as she lay there with her head pressed against the sprinkle of curly hair that covered his broad chest, listening to the steady heartbeat of the man who completed her. In her stubbornness, she'd almost lost him. A lifetime without ever feeling this way again.

She felt him shift, and a soft kiss pressed against the top of her head. "Cal? Are you awake?" she whispered.

"Yes."

She frowned and tried to turn her body to see

his face. There was something strange about the toneless one-word answer. "Are you okay?" Because of the way he held her, all she could see was his stubbled chin.

He sighed with grim determination. As if he'd made a difficult decision. His next words let her know that's exactly what he'd done.

"They're about you."

He spoke so softly, Andrea wasn't certain she'd heard him correctly. "What did you say?"

"The nightmares I've been having for the past several months, they were about you. I'm in the Hadley building and I'm running into the room where I found Marco. I come to this big, gaping hole in the middle of the floor and there you are, just…hanging there by your fingertips." He sighed again, as if reliving the images were exhausting. "I reach out for you…you reach for me, but your fingers slip through mine and then you are falling. I can hear you screaming, I can see the fire below you, and there is not a damn thing I can do about it. That's usually when I wake up."

Andrea broke free of his loose hold and sat up beside him. She stared at his stoic profile in the dark room. He was as still as a statue, and she knew he was awaiting judgment. So, this was the demon that stood between them. Suddenly everything made sense. She should've known it wasn't fear for his own life that was terrorizing Cal. After all, he risked sacrificing himself—*everything* on the job. It was fear for her, or rather, fear of failing her that haunted him.

She reached out and stroked his cheek. "Why didn't you tell me this before?"

He slanted her a glance that made her catch her breath. This confession had cost him more than she realized. There was a look of both hurt and anger in his eyes, and some other unidentifiable emotion, a strange combination she'd never seen before.

"Why? So you would know just how weak I am?"

Andrea rose up on her knees and quickly straddled his lap, taking his face between her hands. "Don't say that. You're not weak!"

Cal simply watched her with hooded eyes, and Andrea knew she had to move carefully: A man's pride was at stake. She braced her small hands on his wide shoulders. "If you're weak because you're afraid of seeing me die in your dreams, then that means that loving me *makes* you weak. Is that what you are saying?"

He turned his head away, pulling free of her hands. "You know that's not it. The problem is not you, it's me. What kind of man cannot control his own mind?"

Her lips twisted thoughtfully. "Cal, considering what you see on a daily basis, charred bodies and destroyed lives, it's amazing you haven't had trouble before now."

"Don't make excuses for me, Andrea. I don't see any more or any less than any other firefighter."

"Oh, really? How many of them do you think watch their fiancée fall to her death on a nightly basis?"

He took her around the waist and lifted her up off of him before standing. "That's not the point."

"Then what is?"

He flopped down on the side of the bed and buried his head in his hands. "This is why I didn't want to tell you about it. Look at me!" He held out his shaking hands. "Just thinking about it does this to me. This is not me! I'm not a—" He just shook his head.

"Not a what? Not a human being?" Andrea put

her arms over his shoulders, feeling the need to touch him, to make herself some part of him. He was hurting so badly, and she didn't have the right words to ease his pain. Nobody did.

Cal pulled her arm forward over his shoulder and kissed the palm of her hand. "I have a confession. I talked Marianne into not canceling the wedding. No cancellation notifications went out."

A stunned silence fell over the room. Andrea felt his muscle tense beneath her arms. She knew he expected her to be angry, he was waiting for her to lash out. But in truth, all she felt was relief that he'd kept her from making the biggest mistake of her life.

"Oh?" She finally managed the one-word answer, while trying to suppress the thrill of excitement that raced up her spine.

"But now I'm wondering if that was such a great idea."

Her heart stopped. "What do you mean?"

"You deserve better than this, Andrea. I don't know exactly what is going on with me, but whatever it is, it won't be solved in a few days' time. And I can't ask you to put your life on hold indefinitely."

"Cal, I only asked one thing of you." She leaned forward and kissed his cheek. "I asked you to share what's going on inside your heart with me, and you just did that. The rest we can work out together."

He stood effectively removing her from him and turned to face her. Andrea sensed that the distance was necessary for whatever he was about to say. "I don't think so, Andrea." There was a coldness to his words that Andrea had never heard before. She was almost certain it was more for his benefit than hers. "You should call Marianne tomorrow. We still have four days, hopefully that will be enough time to cancel everything. I promise not to interfere this time."

Staring at his stiff back, Andrea knew he didn't believe his own words. He didn't want this, he was trying to do what he felt was right. But his right was so wrong. He was about to make the same mistake she'd made out of some sense of noble obligation.

But Cal was stubborn, and when he believed he was right, there was no changing his mind. Watching his rigid stance, Andrea knew nothing she said would change his mind. The time for words had passed. It was time for a leap of faith.

She stood and dressed quickly in the quiet room, trying to ignore the deafening silence between them. When his disregard became unbearable, she spoke to fill the void of space between them. "I'm not calling Marianne," she said softly. "But I will be at the church this Saturday afternoon." She smiled to hide the tears forming in her eyes. Remembering the beautiful wedding she'd planned. "I don't mean to brag, but I look fabulous in my dress. All our family and friends will be there to celebrate with us and wish us well."

Realizing he planned to continue ignoring her, she turned and headed toward the bedroom door. "I will be there, Cal. Waiting for you. The question is…where will you be?"

Cal waited until he heard the front door close before he fell to his knees. He pressed his hands to his face—he could still smell her essence on his fingers. He could still feel her soft, welcoming body beneath him. Taste her sweet kisses.

It wasn't supposed to be this hard! He loved her, she loved him, nothing else should've mattered. But it did matter. The fact that he could not be the man she deserved *mattered!*

It just seemed so damn unfair! After all these

years, to finally find the woman God made just for him and *still* be denied and lose his mind in the process. When he pulled his hands away from his face he was surprised to find water on his palms.

He hadn't cried since he was nine years old. He quickly wiped at his face and climbed to his feet. *Oh, yeah, I'm definitely losing my mind.*

Chapter 18

Cal sat waiting while Mack read the report he'd written up regarding the incident with Jeff Collins. The report was based on everything Cal had seen, and everything that Marco had told him. It all made sense, and now Jeff was home on bail awaiting trial. But still, there was something about the whole incident nagging Cal, but he couldn't put his finger on it. Some part of him hoped Mack might recognize it.

He anxiously glanced at the clock on the wall again. It was 9:38 a.m. on Saturday morning. Andrea was probably awake and getting a shower. He tried not to think about her going to the church for him. He glanced up at his boss standing against his desk, reading the report he'd written up. He glanced at the clock again.

"Looks great, Cal," Mack said when he finally closed the file.

Cal felt slightly disappointed, but hid it. "So, it all makes sense to you?"

Mack smiled. "Yep, everything is neat and in order. Good job, and welcome back."

Cal nodded, unable to shake the sense of foreboding that had haunted him over the past forty-eight hours.

Mack had not been oblivious to Cal's odd behavior, or the fact that Cal was at the firehouse only hours before his wedding. Being one of the invited guests, he knew the ceremony was scheduled to begin in a matter of hours. "Kind of surprised to see you here." He nodded toward the clock on the wall. "Cutting it kind of close, wouldn't you say?"

Cal glanced at his boss. "Yeah." It was all he could manage in his confused state.

Mack stood and prepared to leave. "Well, thanks for getting this report to me so soon."

Cal stood, as well, wondering if he should say

something to Mack about his misgivings, but finally decided against it. "No problem."

Mack was almost out the door when he paused. "I have to say, I'm more than a little shocked by all this. I mean, Jeff was a seasoned veteran, with a hell of a record. Why would he risk it all to frame you?"

Cal shook his head. "I don't know how much of it was to frame me, and how much of it was just being a pyromaniac. Pyros can't help themselves. It's an addiction."

"I know, but still…" Mack huffed. "You'd think a fireman would be better at it. I mean, those first couple of blazes were almost amateurish."

With that statement, Mack disappeared through the door, and missed watching the light come on in Cal's head. That was what had bothered him about this whole thing. It was so damn unprofessional. For someone who knew so much about fire, it seemed almost ridiculous. It was ridiculous.

He grabbed his keys off the desk and headed out the door.

Cal stood in the middle of the burnt-out building, not sure exactly what he was looking for. He heard footsteps, and he swung around to find

Noel moving quietly across the room, headed straight for him.

"What's up, man?" Cal said, trying to sound nonchalant as he mentally worked on an acceptable excuse to explain his presence.

Noel came to a stop right in front of him, looking his friend in the eye. "So…you're having doubts too, huh?"

Cal's eyes widened in surprise. "You, too?"

Noel nodded. "Sorry, man. But it was just too damn tidy for me. I mean anyone who knows as much about fire as Jeff could've come up with a thousand different ways to set blazes, and what happened here was just a little to amateurish for my taste."

Cal was listening intently. "Exactly! I couldn't put my finger on it, but something just didn't seem right, and that's it." He popped his finger. "This was done by someone who is just learning about fire. A beginner."

Noel nodded in agreement. "Problem is, Jeff has already been charged with the crime, so before we can get him released we need to be able to explain what really happened here."

Cal threw up his hands. "Hey, man, you're the expert."

Noel took out his half-empty box of cigarettes and popped one into his hand while his sharp eyes took in their surroundings.

"What happened to the gum?" Cal asked, not at all surprised to see his friend had failed in his latest attempt to quit.

Noel gave a fake shiver. "Just too nasty." He pointed to a far corner of the room. "We know the fire started there, and we have some idea of what kind of accelerant was used."

"Right, right." Cal nodded in agreement and looked in every direction. "I wonder why the arsonist started the fire over there, so far away from the entrance."

Noel crossed the room to where the flames had started in a small huddled corner. "Don't know, does seem odd, though, huh?"

Cal followed, but his eyes were drawn to the window high up on the wall. His mind began to calculate the possibilities. He knew the window was street level, so presumably someone could've come through the window. But Cal knew Noel had originally discounted the possibility because of the size of the opening.

It was in no way large enough for a grown man or even a woman to fit through. But a child...

"What you got?" Noel asked, noticing the thoughtful expression on Cal's face. He followed Cal's eyes to the window. "No way, man. Nobody could get through there."

Cal's eyes slid to his friend, and he decided to keep his suspicions to himself for now. After all, one man was already sitting in prison because of his rush to judgement.

Cal glanced at his watch, and feigned surprise. "Look man, I got to go. But let me know what you find out, okay?" He was already moving in the direction of the door.

"Cal! What you know, Cal?" Noel called after him, knowing he was being left out of something. But Cal was already gone. He glanced back up at the window, trying to figure out what had caught his attention.

He walked closer to the wall, and ran his fingers just above the soot covered counter. That's when he noticed it, and he briefly wondered how he had missed it the first time. But somehow he had, because right there in the soot was a footprint where someone had obviously climbed up on the counter. His fingers floated up went out the window…which was apparently how the arsonist had come in. He looked back at the footprint in the soot once more as his brows crinkled in understanding.

"I'll be damned," he whispered around the still unlit cigarette that dangled precariously from his bottom lip.

Cal stood outside the small Sanchez apartment with his fist half-raised preparing to knock on the door. What he'd come to realize seemed almost impossible but it was the only plausible explanation.

A small part of him wanted to walk away and act like he did not know what he knew, but that would be unfair to the man who'd sat in a jail cell for almost a week for a crime he did not commit.

He shook off his self-doubt and tapped on the door.

Cal could hear Maria answer from inside and he waited patiently for her to come to the door, only then realizing that he'd secretly hoped no one would be home, and he could put off this unpleasant task.

Maria Sanchez swung open the door and stood looking at the large man blocking her doorway. "Cal." She smiled with surprise. "What brings you by?"

"Hi, Maria. Is Marco around?"

She nodded. "Sure, come on in." She stepped aside to let him by. "Marco!" She called in the direction of the bedrooms at the back of the apartment. "Cal is here."

Within seconds, Marco came shooting around the corner, with a full grin wreathing his face. "Cal! What's up, man?" he said as he threw himself into the arms of the giant, and Cal caught him with ease. He hugged him close, again doubting his purpose and mission. What was he doing?

"Hey, little man." He ran a rough hand over Marco's curly head.

"What are you doing here?"

"I need to talk to you." Cal looked down into a small, brown face filled with love and admiration, and he felt like a monster. But he'd chosen his course when he knocked on the door, and there was nothing to do but see it through.

He gently guided the boy over to the couch. "Umm, you remember what you told me about the fire and the man you saw?"

Instantly, Marco's joyful expression faded into a completely blank stare. "Yeah."

Cal gave a nervous glance at Maria, who'd

been standing off to the side the whole while. "Yeah, well, I thought it was Jeff from the firehouse. You remember Jeff, don't you?"

Marco nodded, and frowned. "Yeah, that guy is a real jerk."

"I know." Cal bent forward slightly to be on eye level with Marco. "But he didn't start the fires."

Marco's eyes darted away. "I didn't say a name! I never said Jeff did it." He shook his head defensively.

"I know, I know." Cal laid a calming hand on his small shoulder. "That was my mistake—not yours. It's just when you told me that, all the pieces seem to fall into place, but now I realize I was missing something."

"Cal, just what exactly is this about?" Maria asked, and despite his attempts at delicacy, Cal knew she could sense something was wrong.

As if realizing the truth had been discovered, Marco's head fell, and his whole, thin, little body slumped in defeat.

Cal rubbed the boy's trembling back in an attempt to comfort him, but he spoke to Maria. "I've recently discovered who the real arsonist is, but Marco knew all along." He looked back at his young friend. "Isn't that right, Marco?"

He shook his head rapidly, but never looked up.

Maria moved closer to the pair on the couch. Cal could see she was beginning to understand. Cal knew that this could possibly crush her, but he was obligated to the truth whether he liked it or not.

"And who is the arsonist?" she asked hoarsely.

Before Cal could answer, Marco shot up off the couch like a bullet and pressed his head against her chest as the tears begin to flow. "I'm so sorry, Mama. I'm so sorry."

Maria closed her eyes tightly, and Cal knew instinctively she was trying to close out the truth. She wrapped her arms around her son, and held him close.

Cal just sat on the couch watching a mother and son try to come to grips with a future that was now out of their control. He felt he should say something, but had no words. He couldn't say it would be okay, because he really didn't know if it would be. He couldn't say he understood, because he didn't. So, he just sat silently and waited.

Finally, Maria stepped back from her son, and both faces were streaked with tearstains. She took a deep breath. "So, what now?"

"Honestly, I don't know. I haven't told anyone of my suspicions. I wanted to talk to Marco first."

Maria's brown eyes lit with hope. "Is there any chance…"

Cal shook his head painfully. "I'm sorry, Maria. But I can't *not* report this. An innocent man almost went to jail."

She nodded, and wiped at her face. "I understand." She hugged her son close. "We'll get through this, one way or the other."

Marco wrapped both his arms around his mother's waist, holding on to her like the rock of strength she'd been his whole life.

It gave Cal some comfort in knowing that she would not desert him now. Cal stood and looked down at Marco and felt something in his heart tug. Despite what he'd just done, there was still that look of love and respect in the boy's eyes.

"Cal, I'm really sorry—it's like I couldn't help myself. I'm sorry I disappointed you."

"We all make mistakes," Cal said with a shrug. He knew the words were not what the boy needed to hear, but it was all he was capable of saying. He didn't understand pyros, and doubted that he ever would.

Before he left the small apartment, they all

agreed that Marco should surrender himself to the authorities, instead of Cal reporting him.

Cal gave them Noel's phone number. It eased his conscience a little to put them into the hands of someone he knew and trusted. A few minutes later, as he unlocked his truck door and climbed in, he noticed the two lonely-looking figures standing in the window of the second-floor apartment. He gave a halfhearted wave, and Marco attempted to return it.

Cal considered the events of the past few months, and realized nothing had turned out the way he thought it would. He'd thought becoming chief would fulfill him in some way it had not. And although Jeff was a jerk, he was not an arsonist, and Cal had almost destroyed the man's career. And now, the twelve-year-old boy he thought he knew and understood turned out to be a firebug. And most disconcerting of all, he'd come to discover that he was not indestructible.

Just then, his cell phone rang and he pulled it from his jacket pocket. Seeing the name on the ID caller, he frowned and answered. "Hello?"

"Okay, okay…where are you?" Cal glanced at his watch. It was almost three o'clock, and their wedding was scheduled for four. He still needed to get showered and dressed. But the person on the other end of the phone needed him just as much, if not more. "All right, I'll be there in thirty minutes. Just stay out of sight, okay?"

He sped up to the top speed limit, and hung up the phone as his mind raced in a thousand different directions. He started to call Andrea to let her know that he'd finally come to his senses and had every intention of arriving at the church, but decided to wait until he saw how the situation panned out.

Instead, he called his brother Steve and asked him to meet him at his apartment. Almost six months of preparation and now everything hinged on what happened in the next hour. If he were late, would she wait, or would he risk losing the only woman in the world for him?

He'd known almost from the moment he met her that there was something special about her. But now, almost a year and a half later, he realized how wrong he was about her, as well. He'd seen her as a fragile flower in need of protection and gentle handling.

But over the past several months, she'd proven that she was a lot stronger and tougher than he ever imagined.

Despite everything that had happened, Cal knew with complete certainty that Andrea believed in him. She believed in their love. He took a deep breath, and nodded with certainty. She would wait at the church, just as she waited over the past several months for him to come to terms with everything else going on in his life and his mind.

Yes, she would wait no matter how long it took him to come to her. And when he arrived, she would welcome him with open arms.

Chapter 19

"Hold still." Steve pulled roughly on his brother's necktie.

"Ouch!" Cal yanked back control of his tie. "What are you trying to do? Strangle me?"

Steve turned away. "I should."

Cal focused his attention on tying the necktie, refusing to meet his brother's eyes in the mirror. "I know, I'm an idiot," he mumbled into his shirt.

"Don't have to tell me."

Cal's eyes shot up. "You could try to cut me some slack, man."

"I just hope we're not too late." Steve continued to grumble as he slid his arm into his own jacket. "Why won't you let me call Andrea to let her know we are on our way?"

"I have to make a stop on the way to the church. I wouldn't know when to tell her I was arriving." Cal studied his brother's eyes in the mirror. "By the way, I just wanted to say thanks for trying to talk some sense into me."

"No problem. I know you would do the same for me." Steve placed his hand on Cal's shoulder. "Do you think you will be reinstated?"

Cal gave his brother an unreadable look. "Not until the doc releases me."

"How do you feel about that?"

Cal chuckled. "What's with all this sensitivity stuff?"

Steve frowned. "I know this was one of the things standing between you and Andrea. I'm just wonder—"

Cal held up his hand. "No, the only thing standing between me and Andrea was my own stubborn refusal to admit I needed help. You were right, man. All I needed to do was open my mouth and tell her about it, and when I did…it felt as if the world was being lifted up off my shoulders."

Steve smiled. "I'm proud of you, man."

Cal smiled back with a wink. "Same to you."

Andrea anxiously paced the small cell in the rear of the church, hoping that her actions would be interpreted as impatience by the two women in the room with her, and not the true terror she was feeling in every fiber of her being. The rustling of her gown swooshing across the room only added to the unbearable tension.

"How long are we going to wait here?" Jill interrupted the silence with a high-pitched whine.

"As long as it takes." Marty, who'd been standing by the window watching passing cars, answered.

"Andrea…he's not coming." Jill's voice was filled with sympathy and gentleness. Andrea looked at her cousin in surprise. She'd never really thought of Jill as being sympathetic and gentle.

"You don't know that," Marty hissed. "He could just be running late."

"Hmph," was the only respond Jill gave.

Andrea said nothing to either woman. She had no desire to berate or defend Cal. She'd taken her chances on love, and it had left her standing at the altar alone. Not that she could really blame Cal. After all, she was the one who started this train wreck by running out of the rehearsal the prior week.

Just then the door opened and Dina came into the room. "Okay, I sent Dwight to check the apartment."

Andrea swung in a full circle and the train of her gown flowed around her feet like a white cloud. "What?"

"I thought maybe he got the time wrong."

"You had no right to make that kind of a decision without first consulting me, Dina." Andrea could already feel the mortification of having Cal admit to Dwight that he had no intention of coming to the church.

It was one thing to be stood up at the altar— you could leave with the belief that there was some possible explanation. But to have the missing groom confirm to his best man that he was fully aware that he was missing his own wedding was just too much.

"I can't believe you did that!" Andrea grabbed up the train of her dress and charged toward the door. Feeling the water forming in her eyes, she knew it was time to declare defeat. All she wanted to do at this point was crawl into bed, curl up in a ball and cry her broken heart out for what could've been.

"What'd I do wrong?" Dina asked in confusion looking from Marty to Jill. But it was too late, Andrea was already at the door.

She threw open the wood door and found her path blocked by a shadow. Her wide eyes rose, and rose until they settled on a buck-toothed smile.

"Trying to run out on me?" Cal asked in his typically casual way. As if he'd not left a hundred people hanging in the balance for almost an hour.

Looking into the face of the man she loved, Andrea felt her soul reviving. But that petty part of her that was still bruised by his delay in arriving wanted retribution. "What took you so long?" Her brown eyes narrowed on his face as she glared through the tears.

Cal cupped his index finger and thumb to cradle her chin. "It's not what you think." He smiled, and reached behind him. "I had to stop and pick someone up."

"Mom?" Andrea covered her mouth with both hands, as her mother appeared from behind Cal. "You came." Without thought, she hurled herself forward and into her mother's arms. Suddenly, her body stiffened as another thought occurred to her. "Is Daddy here?"

Margaret wiped clumsily at her own tears as she shook her head. "No, baby. Your father will never change. But I wasn't about to let him make me miss my one and only daughter's wedding. It's bad enough that I was not able to help you plan it."

"Oh, Mom." Andrea hugged her even closer, torn between the little girl inside her that desperately wanted her mother and the woman who knew there would be consequences for her defiance when Margaret returned home. "But I don't want to make things any worse for you."

Margaret smiled back at Cal briefly. "I'm not going back."

Cal braced his large hands on Margaret's shoulder. "Your mom's going to be staying with us for a while. I didn't think you would mind."

Andrea could not hide the joy in her heart as she quickly wiped her face. She wanted to hug her mother, she wanted to hug Cal, she wanted to hug everybody. She wanted to finish getting ready to walk down the aisle and make Cal hers forever. Yes, she finally decided, that was what she wanted most.

She swatted at her eyes and took a deep breath. "Go, go!" she shooed Cal, "everyone is waiting. You have to get to the front of the church before our guests start leaving, and I have to finish getting ready. Get out of here!"

Cal allowed himself to be pushed out of the doorway. "Tyrant," he muttered on a half chuckle. The door slammed in his face. He and Margaret looked at each other in surprise, just as the door was yanked open again.

"Mom, get in here!" Andrea laughed, pulling her mother by the arm through the opening in the door. "I need your help." The door slammed shut again, and Cal was left alone in the hallway.

Cal shook his head, before the door was swung open again. "Wait! I need something borrowed!" Cal studied her excited face, feeling like a king among men, knowing he was the reason for that glow.

She was happy.

Happy that she was about to become his wife. He knew that no matter what would come their way, they would handle it. They had to. This past week had given each a taste of life without the other, and he could not speak for Andrea but it was not a feeling he wanted to experience again.

"Cal! Something borrowed!"

Startled out of his contemplation, Cal began digging around on his person. Finding nothing he thought would satisfy his anxious wife, he glanced at his black onyx class ring he wore constantly. "Here." He pulled and tugged until it came off his finger.

Andrea went to reach for it and he dodged her hand to drop it down the tempting cleavage of her gown.

"Cal!" Andrea laughed and clutched her breast in surprise.

He smiled wickedly and leaned forward. "Don't worry, I'll get it back later." With a wink, he turned and headed toward the sanctuary of the church.

"Cal!"

He stopped at the corner and looked back over his shoulder, the look of pure love in her eyes nearly stopped his heart.

"Thank you," she whispered and the sincerity was written in every fiber of her being. "For everything."

He nodded. "I love you."

She smiled with pure satisfaction. "I love you, too. Now get out there before everyone thinks we've eloped." She blew a kiss and the door slammed shut once more.

A short while later, the couple stood before their collection of family and friends and took their vows.

"Cal, from the first moment I saw you…" Andrea smiled through her tears, "I knew you were what was missing from my life. You were the missing piece of my soul. This past year, things have not always been easy between you and me, but one thing has become certain. I now know that no matter what obstacle we may find in our path, together we can conquer them all."

Cal nodded in complete agreement, and then surprised her by reciting his own original vows. "Andrea, my wife…my life. I tried, really tried to come up with the right words to tell you just how important you are to me." He shook his head in frustration. "But words could never express how important, how *necessary* you are to me. I discovered that for myself just recently when I was forced to contemplate life without you. I don't want to ever experience that again. I can't promise we won't have troubles in the future. All I can say for sure is that no matter what, I will be there with you, by your side, and only God could take me away from you."

Completely unmindful to the laughter of their guests, these witnesses to their commitment of love, Andrea threw herself against Cal with such force, petals from her bouquet of orchids fell to the floor, and his arms closed around her, determined in her mind to hold on to him forever.

Epilogue

Andrea sat on the terrace of the St. John beach-front home, watching as her husband took a forkful of the spicy sausage paella she'd prepared. Cal had commented on the wonderful smell, and made some joke about *her improved cooking* as he passed through the kitchen earlier that afternoon. That comment had earned him a handful of hot peppers tossed into the already tongue-scorching mixture.

Now she watched closely, waiting for the combustion, but it never came. She frowned in confusion as Cal took another bite.

Cal tilted his head at her confused expression. "What's wrong with you?"

She shook her head, and returned her attention to her own meal, deciding that maybe not everyone was sensitive to the spicy seasonings. She should've known Cal would have a stomach like a tank, considering some of the things she'd seen him eat.

Around bite four, she saw his head snap up in surprise, and her devious grin returned. *Finally!*

She heard his breathing become labored and his narrowed eyes honed in on her face. "What the hell did you feed me?"

Unable to hold back any longer, the laughter escaped her throat and she shot up from the table to avoid Cal's sudden lunge in her direction.

Halfway around the table, he turned and rushed into the house. Andrea was feeling quite vindicated for his little prank as she leaned back against the railing watching Cal drink directly from the kitchen sink faucet.

A short while later, he stood in the entrance of the glass double doors, watching Andrea, who was now closely examining her fingernails without a care in the world. A small, smug smile played around her lips. When their eyes met, hers were filled with complete satisfaction.

"You're going to pay for that," he hissed.

She grinned. "Like I told you before, revenge is a dish best served cold." Her eyes shimmered with laugher. "Or in this case, spicy hot."

Recognition dawned in his eyes. "This is because I was late to the church, isn't it?"

She only lifted an eyebrow in response.

He nodded rapidly, as his mind was already working toward retaliation. "Okay, okay, you want to play it like that."

He moved suddenly, but Andrea had been expecting the attack and at the same time, she dodged in the other direction and the chase was on.

By the time Andrea reached the large, elegant dining room, she was realizing she'd made a crucial mistake. She'd assumed because of his size that Cal would be clumsy and have a hard time maneuvering around the elegant furnishing, but he moved through the small spaces as easily as she did. She'd also assumed he would be the first to be winded and give up, but she found she was the one losing steam, while Cal wasn't even breathing hard.

They raced out into the atrium and around the glass-enclosed pool. As the only two people in the large mansion-styled home they literally had the run of the place. But by the time Cal had chased her back into the library, Andrea had given up any hope of losing him and decided to surrender.

She flopped down in a leather chair, and threw up her hands in defeat. "Okay, I give up!" she said through her labored breathing. But Cal just kept coming—with three long strides he was standing beside the chair.

He quirked an eyebrow. "Too bad." He scooped her up in his arms and headed toward the master bedroom. "I'm not taking any prisoners."

Too caught up in laughter and the struggle to regain control of her breathing, Andrea did not even realize they'd reached the bedroom, until she felt herself floating through the air, and then suddenly the soft bed was beneath her and her husband's heavy body was on top of her.

She felt his warm breath on her neck, even as he worked the sundress up her legs.

"Hmm, is this your idea of punishment?" she purred, wrapping her arms around his thick neck.

He lifted the top of his body away from hers so he could reach her front buttons.

"You can call it whatever you want," he murmured as his hungry mouth found its way inside her bra.

Andrea closed her eyes and gave herself over the sensations that were beginning to course through her body. She felt his rough, callused hand slowly working up the inside of her thigh, and subconsciously her legs fell apart.

Settling himself into the seat of her body, Cal pushed up, pressing his rock-hard bulge against her center. He leaned down and covered her mouth with his, running his warm tongue over first her bottom, then top lip, and in response Andrea's mouth opened like a rosebud.

Taking her face between his hands, Cal plunged deep in her mouth, and Andrea knew there was nothing sweeter in the world than the taste of her husband. She wrapped her arms around his large body as tight as she could, trying to pull him closer although it was not physically possible. She needed to feel him inside of her, and she wiggled her bottom suggestively to make her need plain.

Cal propped himself against her shoulder while he worked his jeans down his legs. His erection was standing like a steel blade, more than ready to rend her in half.

"Oh, Cal," she moaned, feeling the thump of hot skin against her opening.

As if it were their own little ritual, Cal answered with, "I know, baby. I know." Unable to wait one moment longer to feel her, he simply pushed her silk panties to the side and slid inside her body, knowing he would receive a warm, wet welcome.

Positioning himself deep inside her, Cal lifted a thigh over each shoulder, and began the long stroking ride to paradise.

Completely open and vulnerable to the assault on her senses, all Andrea could do was moan in pleasure and salute his skill and expertise. "Oh, Cal, please…please…oh…yes, oh yes."

He leaned forward and covered her mouth with his own, imitating the motions of their bodies with his tongue, and Andrea's attention was shifted and torn. She dug her short nails in his shoulder, feeling the pressure build, knowing what was to come, and with Cal it was never anything less than an atomic explosion.

Her head fell back and she broke the connection of their mouths, needing to breathe, but unable to control the sporadic rhythm of her heart. Her head turned side to side, as she felt the climax coming, it was so close…she felt as if she were standing on the edge of a cliff about to go over. The adrenaline pumping through her blood as the penis inside her grew harder still, they were there…close, so close…

"Oh, Cal!" Andrea felt her whole body convulse uncontrollably, her back arched, as she felt the gun go off inside her.

Cal held her pressed close against him as he emptied himself inside her body.

He pressed his head against her neck in concentration, not wanting to miss a second of the temporary bliss. All too soon it was over, and he fell on top of her in exhaustion.

Andrea continued to rain kisses over his face and neck, her hands stroking his sweat-damp body, needing to tell him with her action how complete he made her. How happy he made her. "I love you," she whispered in his ear.

His head shifted as he kissed her gently. "I love you, too." Slowly, gently, he lifted his body from hers. He rolled over onto his back, still holding her tight against his side.

"Thank you for letting my mother stay with us for now." Andrea mumbled against his chest. "Do you think she will be all right while we are away?"

"I don't see why not." He yawned. "Your dad had no idea where I live. As long as she stays around my apartment, she should be find. Did she have the divorce papers served?"

Andrea sighed. "Not yet."

A silence fell over the room as they both recognized the implication of the statement. Despite everything, including her grand gesture of moving out, Margaret was still hesitant to ask for a divorce. They both knew there was a chance she might go back, but neither wanted to admit it out loud.

As he lay there with the woman he loved in his arms, waiting for his heart to slow down, Cal took in the room surrounding them. "I wonder why the St. Johns don't use this place any more than they do. Hell, there are so many of them, you'd think one of them would be here all the time."

Andrea yawned sleepily and shrugged. "I don't know." She was feeling completely sated and satisfied and the last thing she wanted to discuss was why the elegant mansion stood empty most of the time.

"Would you like a house like this one day?"

Andrea was getting very good at understanding her husband, and she could clearly hear the vulnerability in his voice. She propped herself up on his chest, and looked into his soft brown eyes. "I don't care if I spend my life living in a cardboard box…as long as I'm with you."

The gentle smile that came across his face told her she'd said exactly what he needed to hear, and her heart filled with pride.

He huffed. "For a while there, when I was on suspension…"

He shook his head, and she nodded knowingly. "Cal, as long as we have each other, we'll be all right. The rest…" She waved her hand airily. "The rest is just details, and we'll work them out together as we go along. But for now, we both have jobs that provide a good living. So, let's count our blessings and go on."

He nodded slightly, but Andrea understood there was a lot more to it than just income. Cal was born to be a firefighter, it was all he knew and all he wanted, and despite her assurance, without it she really wasn't sure he would've been okay.

But she loved him and that meant loving every part of him, including the parts that terrified her—like his job. Like Dina said, the key was in accepting every day they had together for the blessing it was and not asking for any more than that.

"What do you think will happen to Marco?" she asked, as the thoughts of fire led her mind in the direction of the young boy.

Cal sighed. "I talked to Noel, and they are trying to get him admitted to a juvenile facility that has a good psychiatric department. Because of his age, he will be released when he turns eighteen, but without psychiatric help, he'll probably just be more dangerous than he is now."

"Do you think he is a pyromaniac?"

Cal sighed. "Yes."

She reached up and ran her index finger over the crinkled lines that had appeared on his forehead. "You're worried."

"Yeah, but not about Marco. I mean, I am worried about him, but I know he has Maria to look after him. She's a good mother. What happened is not her fault, and now that she knows about it she'll be watching out. But just now, I was thinking about Jeff."

"Didn't he transfer?"

"Yes, but that's not the point." He folded his arms beneath his head, and Andrea's eyes were immediately drawn to the bunched muscles in his biceps. She felt herself heating up with desire again, but struggled to focus on his words. But it was really hard with all that sex lying right beside her.

Oblivious to her wandering thoughts, Cal continued. "Jeff is the kind of guy who will do anything to get ahead." He chuckled, with little humor. "Look at what he tried to do to me. I don't like the idea of this guy being on anybody's team. He's a walking, talking hazard, not only to himself but anyone unfortunate enough to work with him."

"Then how did he get reinstated?"

Cal shrugged. "Technically, he didn't do anything illegal. Immoral, maybe, but not illegal."

"Is there anything you can do about him?"

"I've done what I could. I filed a report stating my concerns and put it in his permanent record. So at least it will follow him, and maybe his new chief will heed the warning."

Unable to stop her burgeoning lust any longer, Andrea's eyes slid over his exceptional form once more. She sat up and swung a leg over his body so that she was straddling his waist. "Enough talk about ambitious firefighters and pyromaniac little boys. You're giving me the blues." She tugged her dress over her head, pulling her bra along with it.

Cal smiled seductively, as his large hands wrapped around her thighs. "What do you want to do?"

She chuckled. "I thought that was obvious." She reached beneath her and her fingers quickly wrapped around his hardening member and she laughed fully. "You're certainly obvious."

He quirked an eyebrow. "Hell, what did you expect? I have a beautiful, naked woman straddling by body, he's going to react with or without my permission."

She leaned forward and kissed his lips softly. "I have a confession."

"What's that?" he whispered against her lips.

"For a while there, I didn't think we would make it."

He wrapped his hands around her waist, hugging her close. "I know—me, too."

"But now I don't think I could imagine my life without you."

Andrea watched the play of emotions that raced across his face, until his expression became very solemn and his eyes narrowed slightly. "Andrea, I can't promise you it will always be a smooth ride. Quite honestly, I think it will take me some time to get use to this whole married thing. But I can promise you this. I love you. With everything in my soul, I love you and I will do my very best to make sure you never regret marrying me."

Andrea felt a slight shiver race through her body, as she once again imagined receiving *the call,* and in her heart she knew it was not a promise he could keep. But she loved him and would always love him...come what may.

She smiled. "What more could any woman ask for?"

He gave her a knowing grin, and she felt him lift her by the waist and lower her onto the bed.

Her head fell back in pure ecstasy, and she heard herself cooing with pleasure as he pushed deeper inside her body. *Well.* She smiled to herself. *There is always that.*

His
TEMPEST

Favorite author

Candice Poarch

To gain her birthright, Noelle Greenwood assumes
a false identity and plays a risky game of seduction
with Colin Mayes. But when her feelings become
too real, the affair spirals out of control.
Then Colin discovers the truth....

*Available the first week of June
wherever books are sold.*

KIMANI
ROMANCE

www.kimanipress.com

KPCP0200607

ALWAYS *Means* FOREVER

DEBORAH FLETCHER MELLO

Despite her longtime attraction to Darwin Tollins,
Bridget Hinton rejects a casual fling with the notorious
playboy. But when Darwin seeks her legal advice,
he discovers a longing he's never known.
How can he revise Bridget's opinion of him?

*Available the first week of June
wherever books are sold.*

KIMANI
ROMANCE™

KPDFM0210607

Love is always better...

The Second Time Around

Angie Daniels

Visiting her hometown, Brenna Gathers runs into
Jabarie Beaumont, the man who jilted her at the altar
years ago. Convinced by his father Brenna was a
gold digger, Jabarie never got her out of his system.
Now he's on a mission to win Brenna's heart
a second time.

*Available the first week of June
wherever books are sold.*

KIMANI™
ROMANCE

Acclaimed author

Adrianne Byrd

BlueSkies

Part of Arabesque's At Your Service military miniseries.

Fighter pilot Sydney Garret was born to fly.
No other thrill came close—until Captain James Colton
ignited in her a reckless passion that led to their short-
lived marriage. When they parted, Sydney knew fate
would somehow reunite them. But no one imagined it
would be a matter of life or death....

"Byrd proves once again that she's
a wonderful storyteller."
—*Romantic Times BOOKreviews* on
THE BEAUTIFUL ONES

Coming the first week of June
wherever books are sold.

ARABESQUE®

www.kimanipress.com   KPAB0120607

"Like fine wine, Gwynne Forster's storytelling skills get better over time. Drama, family struggles, passion and true-to-life characters make Forster's latest her best yet."
—Donna Hill, author of GETTING HERS

BESTSELLING AUTHOR

GWYNNE
Forster

HOT
Entertainment
SERIES

Just the Man She Needs

Felicia Parker is a successful New York columnist with a Rolodex full of celebrity connections—but zero social contacts. So when a glitzy event requires bringing a date, she hires stunningly handsome, high-powered CEO John Ashton Underwood. Their worlds clash, but the scorching attraction between them could burn up the pages....

Coming the first week of June
wherever books are sold.

ARABESQUE®

www.kimanipress.com

KPGF0130607

A brand-new Kendra Clayton mystery
from acclaimed author…

ANGELA HENRY

Diva's Last Curtain Call

Amateur sleuth Kendra Clayton finds herself immersed in
mayhem once again when a cunning killer rolls credits on a
fading movie star. Kendra's publicity-seeking sister is pegged
as the prime suspect, but Kendra knows her sister is no
murderer. She soon uncovers some surprising Hollywood
secrets, putting herself in danger of becoming the killer's
encore performance....

"A tightly woven mystery."
—*Ebony* magazine on *The Company You Keep*

sepia™

*Coming the first
week of June
wherever books
are sold.*

www.kimanipress.com

KPAH0440607